PRAISE FOR URSULA K. LE GUIN'S

Changing Planes

"Even Le Guin's overtly cautionary tales have a delicacy that disarms resistance. Outstanding among these are the almost unbearably poignant 'Fliers of Gy' and 'The Island of the Immortals,' which break new ground in exploring the dangers of getting what you wish for."

—*The New York Times Book Review*

"Wry and exhilarating . . . perhaps the most thoroughly enjoyable—and certainly the funniest—of all Le Guin's collections to date . . . veers effortlessly from Borgesian *ficciones* to Swiftian satire to more fully developed but still satirical SF conceits." —*Gary K. Wolfe, Locus*

"Speculative fiction master Le Guin explores assumptions about our own world. The stories fit well together as a meditation on culture and what it means to be human . . . Le Guin's writing is deceptively simple, but she's working with deep themes, including the prevalence of violence, the tension between science and nature, and how we need to fight fear and sometimes risk ourselves in order to feel truly alive. A humorous, imaginative, and thoughtful collection." —*Library Journal*

"A delight." —*Publishers Weekly*

"Vivid . . . With dispassion, wry humor, and a keen eye . . . [Le Guin] describes those excursions in hopes of inducing the reader to try interplanetary travel. Sure to delight fans of the unusual travelogue, this is just plain good airport reading." —*Booklist*

The Other Wind

"The magic of Earthsea is primal; the lessons of Earthsea remain as potent, as wise, and as necessary as anyone could dream."

—Neil Gaiman

"A quiet, well-told tale . . . another solid entry in a very good fantasy series." —*Orlando Sentinel*

continued . . .

"One of the few writers I know who excels at both political fiction and epic fantasy. She's brilliant at both." —Salon.com

"Le Guin is not only one of the purest stylists writing in English, but the most transcendently truthful of writers." —*The Nation*

"Le Guin remains a master of subtlety and grace as she finds new and surprising ways to express deep truths cloaked in the trappings of fantasy." —*Library Journal*

Tales from Earthsea

"Earthsea's magic serves as a metaphor for the writer's own sorcery . . . Memorable." —*The New York Times Book Review*

"A writer of depth who recognizes that not all fantasy venues are created equal . . . Le Guin's combination of opaque simplicity and transparent complexity . . . make for stories that stand shoulder to shoulder with ancient archetypal fairy tales and fables." —*The Washington Post Book World*

"In the canon of great adult fantasy literature, right next to Tolkien . . . If you've had enough of Harry Potter–style kid-wizardry, Le Guin offers a powerful tonic. These tales are intense, moving, engaging, and best of all, character-driven: Le Guin knows people, wizards or not." —*The Boulder Daily Camera*

"*Tales from Earthsea* . . . has poetry and true magic. Furthermore, it has a great writer's love of an imaginary land that once existed only in her mind and now exists as a treasure in the real world for all lovers of fantasy, today and tomorrow and forever." —*Orlando Sentinel*

"A treasure . . . at the top of any list of fantasy to be cherished." —Andre Norton

"Le Guin hasn't lost her touch. She draws us into the magical land and its inhabitants' doings immediately. Earthsea mavens must rejoice, and relative newcomers will profit from the Earthsea history and two maps that round out the book." —*Booklist*

CHANGING
PLANES

URSULA K. LE GUIN

Illustrations by Eric Beddows

ACE BOOKS, NEW YORK

An Ace Book
Published by The Berkley Publishing Group
A division of Penguin Group (USA) Inc.
375 Hudson Street
New York, New York 10014

PRINTING HISTORY
Harcourt Books hardcover edition / July 2003
Ace trade paperback edition / August 2004

Library of Congress Cataloging-in-Publication Data

Le Guin, Ursula K., 1929–
   Changing planes / Ursula K. Le Guin ; illustrations by Eric Beddows.— Ace
trade pbk. ed.
      p. cm.
   ISBN 0-441-01156-X
   1. Fantasy fiction, American. 2. Imaginary societies. 3. Voyages, Imaginary.
I. Title.

PS3562.E42C48 2004
813'.54—dc22

2004046109

CONTENTS

Author's Note   ix

Sita Dulip's Method   1

Porridge on Islac   7

The Silence of the Asonu   19

Feeling at Home with the Hennebet   30

The Ire of the Veksi   41

Seasons of the Ansarac   52

Social Dreaming of the Frin   76

The Royals of Hegn   89

Woeful Tales from Mahigul   106

Great Joy   133

Wake Island   150

The Nna Mmoy Language   165

The Building   180

The Fliers of Gy   194

The Island of the Immortals   213

Confusions of Uñi   228

Author's Note

This book was written when the miseries of air travel seemed to be entirely the doing of the corporations that ran the airports and the airlines, without any help from bigots with beards in caves. Spoofing the whole thing was easy. They were mere discomforts, after all. Things have changed, but the principle on which Sita Dulip's Method is founded remains valid. Error, fear, and suffering are the mothers of invention. The constrained body knows and values the freedom of the mind.

Sita Dulip's Method

⁓

The range of the airplane—a few thousand miles, the other side of the world, coconut palms, glaciers, the poles, the Poles, a lama, a llama, etc.—is pitifully limited compared to the vast extent and variety of experience provided, to those who know how to use it, by the airport.

Airplanes are cramped, jammed, hectic, noisy, germy, alarming, and boring, and they serve unusually nasty food at utterly unreasonable intervals. Airports, though larger, share the crowding, vile air, noise, and relentless tension, while their food is often even nastier, consisting entirely of fried lumps of something; and the places one has to eat it in are suicidally depressing. On the airplane, everyone is locked into a seat with a belt and can move only during very short periods when they are allowed to stand in line waiting to empty their bladders until, just before they reach the toilet cubicle, a nagging loudspeaker harries them back to belted immobility. In the airport, luggage-laden people rush hither and yon through endless corridors, like souls to each of whom the devil has furnished a different, inaccurate map of the escape route from hell. These rushing people are watched by people who sit in plastic seats bolted to the floor and who might just as well be bolted to the seats. So far, then, the airport and the airplane are equal, in the way that the bottom of one septic tank is equal, all in all, to the bottom of the next septic tank.

If both you and your plane are on time, the airport is merely a diffuse, short, miserable prelude to the intense, long, miserable plane trip. But what if there's five hours between your arrival and your connecting flight, or your plane is late arriving and you've missed your connection, or the connecting flight is late, or the staff of another airline are striking for a wage-benefit package and the government has not yet ordered out the National Guard to control this threat to international capitalism so your airline staff is trying to handle twice as many people as usual, or there are tornadoes or thunderstorms or blizzards or little important bits of the plane missing or any of the thousand other reasons (never under any circumstances the fault of the airlines, and rarely explained at the time) why those who go places on airplanes sit and sit and sit and sit in airports, not going anywhere?

In this, probably its true aspect, the airport is not a prelude to travel, not a place of transition: it is a stop. A blockage. A constipation. The airport is where you can't go anywhere else. A nonplace in which time does not pass and there is no hope of any meaningful existence. A terminus: the end. The airport offers

nothing to any human being except access to the interval between planes.

It was Sita Dulip of Cincinnati who first realised this, and so discovered the interplanar technique most of us now use.

Her connecting flight from Chicago to Denver had been delayed by some unspeakable, or at any rate untold, malfunction of the airplane. It was listed as departing at 1:10, two hours late. At 1:55, it was listed as departing at 3:00. It was then taken off the departures list. There was no one at the gate to answer questions. The lines at the desks were eight miles long, only slightly shorter than the lines at the toilets. Sita Dulip had eaten a nasty lunch standing up at a dirty plastic counter, since the few tables were all occupied by wretched, whimpering children with savagely punitive parents, or by huge, hairy youths wearing shorts, tank tops, and rubber thongs. She had long ago read the editorials in the local newspaper, which advocated using the education budget to build more prisons and applauded the recent tax break for citizens whose income surpassed that of Rumania. The airport bookstores did not sell books, only bestsellers, which Sita Dulip cannot read without risking a severe systemic reaction. She had been sitting for over an hour on a blue plastic chair with metal tubes for legs bolted to the floor in a row of people sitting in blue plastic chairs with metal tubes for legs bolted to the floor facing a row of people sitting in blue plastic chairs with metal tubes for legs bolted to the floor, when (as she later said), "It came to me."

She had discovered that, by a mere kind of twist and a slipping bend, easier to do than to describe, she could go anywhere—be anywhere—because she was *already between planes*.

She found herself in Strupsirts, that easily accessible and

picturesque though somewhat three-dimensional region of waterspouts and volcanoes, still a favorite with beginning interplanary travelers. In her inexperience she was nervous about missing her flight and stayed only an hour or two before returning to the airport. She saw at once that, on this plane, her absence had taken practically no time at all.

Delighted, she slipped off again and found herself in Djeyo. She spent two nights at a small hotel run by the Interplanary Agency, with a balcony overlooking the amber Sea of Somue. She went for long walks on the beach, swam in the chill, buoyant, golden water—"like swimming in brandy and soda," she said—and got acquainted with some pleasant visitors from other planes. The small and inoffensive natives of Djeyo, who take no interest in anyone else and never come down to the ground, squatted high in the crowns of the alm-palms, bargaining, gossiping, and singing soft, quick love songs to one another. When she reluctantly returned to the airport to check up, nine or ten minutes had passed. Her flight was soon called.

She flew to Denver to her younger sister's wedding. On the flight home she missed her connection at Chicago and spent a week on Choom, where she has often returned since. Her job with an advertising agency involves a good deal of air travel, and by now she speaks Choomwot like a native.

Sita taught several friends, of whom I am happy to be one, how to change planes. And so the technique, the method, has gradually spread out from Cincinnati. Others on our plane may well have discovered it for themselves, since it appears that a good many people now practice it, not always intentionally. One meets them here and there.

While staying with the Asonu I met a man from the Candensian plane, which is very much like ours, only more of it consists of Toronto. He told me that in order to change planes all a Candensian has to do is eat two dill pickles, tighten his belt, sit upright in a hard chair with his back not touching the back, and breathe ten times a minute for about ten minutes. This is enviably easy, compared to our technique. We (I mean people from the plane I occupy when not traveling) seem unable to change planes except at airports.

The Interplanary Agency long ago established that a specific combination of tense misery, indigestion, and boredom is the essential facilitator of interplanary travel; but most people, from most planes, don't have to suffer the way we do.

The following reports and descriptions of other planes, given me by friends or written from notes I made on my own excursions and in libraries of various kinds, may induce the reader to try interplanary travel; or if not, they may at least help to pass an hour in an airport.

Porridge on Islac

It must be admitted that the method invented by Sita Dulip is not entirely reliable. You sometimes find yourself on a plane that isn't the one you meant to go to. If whenever you travel you carry with you a copy of Rornan's *Handy Planary Guide,* you can read up on wherever it is you get to when you get there, though Rornan is not always reliable either. But the *Encyclopedia Planaria,* in forty-four volumes, is not portable, and after all, what is entirely reliable unless it's dead?

I arrived on Islac unintentionally, when I was inexperienced, before I had learned to tuck Rornan into my suitcase. The Interplanary Hotel there did have a set of the *Encyclopedia,* but it was at the bindery, because, they said, the bears had eaten the glue in the bindings and the books had all come to pieces. I

7

thought they must have rather odd bears on Islac, but did not like to ask about them. I looked around the halls and my room carefully in case any bears were lurking. It was a beautiful hotel and the hosts were pleasant, so I decided to take my luck as it came and spend a day or two on Islac. I got to looking over the books in the bookcase in my room and trying out the built-in legemat, and had quite forgotten about bears, when something scuttled behind a bookend.

I moved the bookend and glimpsed the scuttler. It was dark and furry but had a long, thin tail of some kind, almost like wire. It was six or eight inches long not counting the tail. I didn't much like sharing my room with it, but I hate complaining to strangers—you can only complain satisfactorily to people you know really well—so I moved the heavy bookend over the hole in the wall the creature had disappeared into, and went down to dinner.

The hotel served family style, all the guests at one long table. They were a friendly lot from several different planes. We were able to converse in pairs using our translatomats, though general conversation overloaded the circuits. My left-hand neighbor, a rosy lady from a plane she called Ahyes, said she and her husband came to Islac quite often. I asked her if she knew anything about the bears here.

"Yes," she said, smiling and nodding. "They're quite harmless. But what little pests they are! Spoiling books, and licking envelopes, and snuggling in the bed!"

"Snuggling in the bed?"

"Yes, yes. They were pets, you see."

Her husband leaned forward to talk to me around her. He

was a rosy gentleman. "Teddy bears," he said in English, smiling. "Yes."

"Teddy bears?"

"Yes, yes," he said, and then had to resort to his own language—"teddy bears are little animal pets for children, isn't that right?"

"But they're not live animals."

He looked dismayed. "Dead animals?"

"No—stuffed animals—toys—"

"Yes, yes. Toys, pets," he said, smiling and nodding.

He wanted to talk about his visit to my plane; he had been to San Francisco and liked it very much, and we talked about earthquakes instead of teddy bears. He had found a 5.6 earthquake "a very charming experience, very enjoyable," and he and his wife and I laughed a great deal as he told about it. They were certainly a nice couple, with a positive outlook.

When I went back to my room I shoved my suitcase up against the bookend that blocked the hole in the wall, and lay in bed hoping that the teddy bears did not have a back door.

Nothing snuggled into the bed with me that night. I woke very early, being jet-lagged by flying from London to Chicago, where my westbound flight had been delayed, allowing me this vacation. It was a lovely warm morning, the sun just rising. I got up and went out to take the air and see the city of Slas on the Islac plane.

It might have been a big city on my plane, nothing exotic to my eye, except the buildings were more mixed in style and in size than ours. That is, we put the big imposing buildings at the center and on the nice streets, and the small humble ones in the neighborhoods or barrios or slums or shantytowns. In this residential quarter of Slas, big houses were all jumbled up together with tiny cottages, some of them hardly bigger than hutches. When I went the other direction, downtown, I found the same wild variation of scale in the office buildings. A massive old four-story granite block towered over a ten-story building ten feet wide, with floors only five or six feet apart—a doll's skyscraper. By then, however, enough Islai were out and about that the buildings didn't puzzle me as much as the people did.

They were amazingly various in size, in color, in shape. A woman who must have been eight feet tall swept past me, literally: she was a street sweeper, busily and gracefully clearing the sidewalk of dust. She had what I took to be a spare broom or duster, a great spray of feathers, tucked into her waistband in back like an ostrich's tail. Next came a businessman striding along, hooked up to the computer network via a plug in his ear, a mouthpiece, and the left frame of his spectacles, talking away as he studied the market report. He came up about to my waist. Four young men passed on the other side of the street; there was nothing odd about them except that they all looked exactly alike. Then came a child trotting to school with his little backpack. He trotted on all fours, neatly, his hands in leather mitts or boots that protected them from the pavement; he was pale, with small eyes, and a snout, but he was adorable.

A sidewalk café had just opened up beside a park downtown. Though ignorant of what the Islai ate for breakfast, I was ravenous, ready to dare anything edible. I held out my translatomat to the waitress, a worn-looking woman of forty or so with nothing unusual about her, to my eye, but the beauty of her thick, yellow, fancifully braided hair. "Please tell me what a foreigner eats for breakfast," I said.

She laughed, then smiled a beautiful, kind smile, and said, via the translatomat, "Well, *you* have to tell me that. We eat cledif, or fruit with cledif."

"Fruit with cledif, please," I said, and presently she brought me a plate of delicious-looking fruits and a large bowl of pale yellow gruel, smooth, about as thick as very heavy cream, lukewarm. It sounds ghastly, but it was delicious—mild but subtle, lightly filling and slightly stimulating, like café au lait. She waited to see if I liked it. "I'm sorry, I didn't think to ask if you were a carnivore," she said. "Carnivores have raw cullis for breakfast, or cledif with offal."

"This is fine," I said.

Nobody else was in the place, and she had taken a liking to me, as I had to her. "May I ask where you come from?" she asked, and so we got to talking. Her name was Ai Li A Le. I soon realised she was not only an intelligent person but a highly educated one. She had a degree in plant pathology—but was lucky, she said, to have a job as a waitress. "Since the Ban," she said, shrugging. When she saw that I didn't know what the Ban was, she was about to tell me; but several customers were sitting down now, a great bull of a man at one table, two mousy girls at another, and she had to go wait on them.

"I wish we could go on talking," I said, and she said, with her kind smile, "Well, if you come back at sixteen, I can sit and talk with you."

"I will," I said, and I did. After wandering around the park and the city I went back to the hotel for lunch and a nap, then

took the monorail back downtown. I never saw such a variety of people as were in that car—all shapes, sizes, colors, degrees of hairiness, furriness, featheriness (the street sweeper's tail had indeed been a tail) and, I thought, looking at one long, greenish youth, even leafiness. Surely those were fronds over his ears? He was whispering to himself as the warm wind swept through the car from the open windows.

The only thing the Islai seemed to have in common, unfortunately, was poverty. The city certainly had been prosperous once, not very long ago. The monorail was a snazzy bit of engineering, but it was showing wear and tear. The surviving old buildings—which were on a scale I found familiar—were grand but run-down, and crowded by the more recent giant's houses and doll's houses and buildings like stables or mews or rabbit hutches—a terrible hodgepodge, all of it cheaply built, rickety-looking, shabby. The Islai themselves were shabby, when they weren't downright ragged. Some of the furrier and featherier ones were clothed only by their fur and feathers. The green boy wore a modesty apron, but his rough trunk and limbs were bare. This was a country in deep, hard economic trouble.

Ai Li A Le was sitting at one of the outside tables at the café (the cledifac) next door to the one where she waited tables. She smiled and beckoned to me, and I sat down with her. She had a small bowl of chilled cledif with sweet spices, and I ordered the same. "Please tell me about the Ban," I asked her.

"We used to look like you," she said.

"What happened?"

"Well," she said, and hesitated. "We like science. We like engineering. We are good engineers. But perhaps we are not very good scientists."

To summarise her story: the Islai had been strong on practical physics, agriculture, architecture, urban development, engineering, invention, but weak in the life sciences, history, and theory. They had their Edisons and Fords but no Darwin, no Mendel. When their airports got to be just like ours, if not worse, they began to travel between planes; and on some plane, about a hundred years ago, one of their scientists discovered applied genetics. He brought it home. It fascinated them. They promptly mastered its principles. Or perhaps they had not quite mastered them before they started applying them to every life-form within reach.

"First," she said, "to plants. Altering food plants to be more fruitful, or to resist bacteria and viruses, or to kill insects, and so on."

I nodded. "We're doing a good deal of that too," I said.

"Really? Are you..." She seemed not to know how to ask the question she wanted to ask. "I'm corn, myself," she said at last, shyly.

I checked the translatomat. Uslu: corn, maize. I checked the dictionary, and it said that uslu on Islac and maize on my plane were the same plant.

I knew that the odd thing about corn is that it has no wild form, only a distant wild ancestor that you'd never recognise as corn. It's entirely a construct of long-term breeding by ancient gatherers and farmers. An early genetic miracle. But what did it have to do with Ai Li A Le?

Ai Li A Le with her wonderful, thick, gold-colored, corn-colored hair cascading in braids from a topknot...

"Only four percent of my genome," she said. "There's about half a percent of parrot, too, but it's recessive. Thank God."

I was still trying to absorb what she had told me. I think she felt her question had been answered by my astonished silence.

"They were utterly irresponsible," she said severely. "With all their programs and policies and making everything better, they were fools. They let all kinds of things get loose and inter-breed. Wiped out rice in one decade. The improved breeds went sterile. The famines were terrible...Butterflies, we used to have butterflies, do you have them?"

"Some, still," I said.

"And deletu?" A kind of singing firefly, now extinct, said my translatomat. I shook my head wistfully.

She shook her head wistfully.

"I never saw a butterfly or a deletu. Only pictures...The in-secticidal clones got them...But the scientists learned nothing—nothing! They set about improving the animals. Improving us! Dogs that could talk, cats that could play chess! Human beings who were going to be all geniuses and never get sick and live five hundred years! They did all that, oh yes, they did all that. There are talking dogs all over the place, unbelievably boring they are, on and on and on about sex and shit and smells, and smells and shit and sex, and do you love me, do you love me, do you love me. I can't stand talking dogs. My big poodle Rover, he never says a word, the dear good soul. And then the humans! We'll never, ever get rid of the Premier. He's a Healthy, a bloody

GAPA. He's ninety now and looks thirty and he'll go on looking thirty and being premier for four more centuries. He's a pious hypocrite and a greedy, petty, stupid, mean-minded crook. Just the kind of man who ought to be siring children for five centuries...The Ban doesn't apply to him...But still, I'm not saying the Ban was wrong. They had to do something. Things were really awful, fifty years ago. When they realised that genetic hackers had infiltrated all the laboratories, and half the techs were Bioist fanatics, and the Godsone Church had all those secret factories in the eastern hemisphere deliberately turning out genetic melds...Of course most of those products weren't viable. But a lot of them were...The hackers were so good at it. The chicken people, you've seen them?"

As soon as she asked, I realised that I had: short, squat people who ran around in intersections squawking, so that all the traffic gridlocked in an effort not to run them over. "They just make me want to cry," Ai Li A Le said, looking as if she wanted to cry.

"So the Ban forbade further experimentation?" I asked.

She nodded. "Yes. Actually, they blew up the laboratories. And sent the Bioists for reeducation in the Gubi. And jailed all the Godsone Fathers. And most of the Mothers too, I guess. And shot the geneticists. And destroyed all the experiments in progress. And the products, if they were"—she shrugged—"'too far from the norm.' The norm!" She scowled, though her sunny face was not made for scowling. "We don't have a norm anymore. We don't have species any more. We're a genetic porridge. When we plant maize, it comes up weevil-repellent clover that smells like chlorine. When we plant an oak, it comes up poison oak fifty feet high with a ten-foot-thick trunk. And when we make love we don't know if we're going to have a baby, or a foal, or a cygnet, or a sapling. My daughter—" and she paused. Her face worked and she had to compress her lips before she could go on. "My daughter lives in the North Sea. On raw fish. She's very beautiful. Dark and silky and beautiful. But—I had to take her to the seacoast when she was two years old. I had to put her in that cold water, those big waves. I had to let her swim away, let her go be what she is. But she is human too! She is, she is human too!"

She was crying, and so was I.

After a while, Ai Li A Le went on to tell me how the Genome Collapse had led to profound economic depression, only worsened by the Purity Clauses of the Ban, which restricted jobs in the professions and government to those who tested 99.44% human—with exceptions for Healthies, Righteous Ones, and other GAPAs (Genetically Altered Products Approved by the Emergency Government). This was why she was working as a waitress. She was four percent maize.

"Maize was once the holy plant of many people, where I come from," I said, hardly knowing what I said. "It is such a beautiful plant. I love everything made out of corn—polenta, hoecake, cornbread, tortillas, canned corn, creamed corn, hominy, grits, corn whiskey, corn chowder, on the cob, tamales—it's all good. All good, all kind, all sacred. I hope you don't mind if I talk about eating it!"

"Heavens no," said Ai Li A Le, smiling. "What did you think cledif was made from?"

After a while I asked her about teddy bears. That phrase of course meant nothing to her, but when I described the creature in my bookcase she nodded—"Oh yes! Bookbears. Early on, when the genetic designers were making everything better, you know, they dwarfed bears way down for children's pets. Like toys, stuffed animals, only they were alive. Programmed to be passive and affectionate. But some of the genes they used for dwarfing came from insects—springtails and earwigs. And the bears began to eat the children's books. At night, while they were supposed to be cuddling in bed with the children, they'd go eat their books. They like paper and glue. And when they bred, the offspring had long tails, like wires, and a sort of insect jaw, so they weren't much good for the children anymore. But by then they'd escaped into the woodwork, between the walls... Some people call them bearwigs."

I have been back to Islac several times to see Ai Li A Le. It is not a happy plane, or a reassuring one, but I would go to worse places than Islac to see so kind a smile, such a topknot of gold, and to drink maize with the woman who is maize.

The Silence of the Asonu

The silence of the Asonu is proverbial. The first visitors to their plane believed that these gracious, gracile people were mute, lacking any language other than that of gesture, expression, and gaze. Later, hearing Asonu children chatter, the visitors suspected that among themselves the adults spoke, keeping silence only with strangers. We know now that the Asonu are not dumb, but that once past early childhood they speak very rarely to anyone, under any circumstances. They do not write; and unlike mutes, or monks under vows of silence, they do not use any signs or other devices in place of speaking.

This nearly absolute abstinence from language makes them fascinating.

People who live with animals value the charm of muteness. It can be a real pleasure to know when the cat walks into the room that he won't mention any of your shortcomings, or that you can tell your grievances to your dog without his repeating them to the people who caused them.

Those who can't talk, and those who can talk but don't, have the great advantage over the rest of us in that they never say anything stupid. This may be why we are convinced that if they spoke they would have something wise to say.

Thus there has come to be considerable tourist traffic to the Asonu. Having a strong tradition of hospitality, the Asonu entertain their visitors with generosity and courtesy, though without modifying their own customs.

Some tourists go there simply in order to join the natives in their silence, grateful to spend a few weeks where they do not have to festoon and obscure every human meeting with verbiage. Many such visitors, having been accepted into a household as a paying guest, return year after year, forming bonds of unspoken affection with their quiet hosts.

Others follow their Asonu guides or hosts about, talking to them hour after hour, confiding their whole life to them, in rapture at having at last found a listener who won't interrupt or comment or mention that his cousin had an even larger tumor than that. As such people usually know little Asonu and speak entirely in their own language, they evidently aren't worried by the question that vexes some visitors: Since the Asonu don't talk, do they, in fact, listen?

They certainly hear and understand what is said to them in their own language, since they're prompt to respond to their

children, to indicate directions by gesture to the halting and mis-
pronounced inquiries of tourists, and to leave a building at the
cry of "Fire!" But the question remains, do they listen to discur-
sive speech and sociable conversation, or do they merely hear it
while keeping silently attentive to something beyond speech?
Their amiable and apparently easy manner seems to some observers the placid surface of a deep preoccupation, a constant
alertness, like that of a mother who while entertaining her guests
or seeing to her husband's comfort is listening every moment for
the cry of her baby in another room.

To perceive the Asonu thus is almost inevitably to interpret
their silence as a concealment. As they grow up, it seems, they
cease to speak because they are listening to something we do not
hear, a secret which their silence hides.

Some visitors to their world are convinced that the lips of
these quiet people are locked upon a knowledge which, in pro-
portion as it is hidden, must be valuable—a spiritual treasure,
a speech beyond speech, possibly even that ultimate revelation
promised by so many religions, and indeed frequently delivered, but never in a wholly communicable form. The tran-
scendent knowledge of the mystic cannot be expressed in
language. It may be that the Asonu avoid language for this
very reason.

It may be that they keep silence because if they spoke, everything of importance would have been said.

Believers in the Wisdom of the Asonu have followed individuals about for years, waiting for the rare words they speak, writing them down, saving them, studying them, arranging and
collating them, finding arcane meanings and numerical corre-

spondences in them, in search of the hidden message. To some, however, these utterances do not seem to be as momentous as one might expect from their rarity. They might even be described as banal.

There is no written form of the Asonu language, and translation of speech is considered to be so uncertain that translatomats aren't issued to the tourists, most of whom don't want them anyway. Those who wish to learn Asonu can do so only by listening to and imitating children, who by six or seven years old are already becoming unhappy when asked to talk.

Here are the Eleven Sayings of the Elder of Isu, collected over four years by a devotee from Ohio, who had already spent six years learning the language from the children of the Isu Group. Months of silence occurred between most of these statements, and two years between the fifth and sixth.

1. Not there.

2. It is almost ready [or] Be ready for it soon.

3. Unexpected!

4. It will never cease.

5. Yes.

6. When?

7. It is very good.

8. Perhaps.

9. Soon.

10. Hot! [or] Very warm!

11. It will not cease.

The devotee wove these eleven sayings into a coherent spiritual statement or testament which he understood the Elder to have been making, little by little, during the last four years of his life. The Ohio Reading of the Sayings of the Elder of Isu is as follows:

(1) What we seek is not in any object or experience of our mortal life. We live among appearances, on the verge of the Spiritual Truth. (2) We must be as ready for it as it is ready for us, for (3) it will come when we least expect it. Our perception of the Truth is sudden as a lightning flash, but (4) the Truth itself is eternal and unchanging. (5) Indeed we must positively and hopefully, in a spirit of affirmation, (6) continually ask when, when shall we find what we seek? (7) For the Truth is the medicine for our soul, the knowledge of absolute goodness. (8, 9) It may come very soon. Perhaps it is coming even now in this moment. (10) Its warmth and brightness are as those of the sun, but the sun will perish (11) and the Truth will not perish. Never will the warmth, the brightness, the goodness of the Truth cease or fail us.

Another interpretation of the Sayings may be made by referring to the circumstances in which the Elder spoke, faithfully recorded by the devotee from Ohio, whose patience was equaled only by the Elder's:

1. Spoken in an undertone as the Elder looked through a chest of clothing and ornaments.

2. Spoken to a group of children on the morning of a ceremony.

3. Said with a laugh in greeting the Elder's younger sister, returned from a long trip.

4. Spoken the day after the burial of the Elder's sister.

5. Said while embracing the Elder's brother-in-law some days after the funeral.

6. Asked of an Asonu "doctor" who was making a "spirit-body" drawing in white and black sand for the Elder. These drawings seem to be both curative and diagnostic, but we know very little about them. The observer states that the doctor's answer was a short curving line drawn outward from the navel of the spirit-body figure. This, however, may be only the observer's reading of what was not an answer at all.

7. Said to a child who had woven a reed mat.

8. Spoken in answer to a young grandchild who asked, "Will you be at the big feast, Grandmother?"

9. Spoken in answer to the same child, who asked, "Are you going to be dead like Great-Auntie?"

10. Said to a baby who was toddling towards a firepit where the flames were invisible in the sunlight.

11. Last words, spoken the day before the Elder's death.

The last six Sayings were all spoken in the last half year of the Elder's life, as if the approach of death had made the Elder positively loquacious. Five of the Sayings were spoken to, or in at least in the presence of, young children who were still at the talking stage.

Speech from an adult must be very impressive to an Asonu child. Like the foreign linguists, Asonu babies learn the language by listening to older children. The mother and other adults encourage the child to speak only by attentive listening and prompt, affectionate, wordless response.

The Asonu live in close-knit, extended-family groups, in frequent contact with other groups. Their pasturing life, following the great flocks of anamanu which furnish them wool, leather, milk, and meat, leads them on a ceaseless seasonal nomadic circuit within a vast shared territory of mountains and foothills. Families frequently leave their groups to go wandering and visiting. At the great festivals and ceremonies of healing and renewal many groups come together for days or weeks, exchanging hospitality. No hostile relations between groups are apparent, and in fact no observer has reported seeing adult Asonu fight or quarrel. Arguments clearly are out of the question.

Children from two to six years old chatter to each other constantly; they argue, wrangle, bicker, quarrel, and sometimes come to blows. As they reach six or seven they begin to speak less and quarrel less. By the time they are eight or nine most of them are very shy of words and reluctant to answer a question except by gesture. They have learned to quietly evade inquiring tourists and linguists with notebooks and recording devices. By adolescence they are as silent and as peaceable as the adults.

Children between eight and twelve do most of the looking after the younger ones. All the sub-adolescent children of the family group go about together, and in such groups the two-to-six-year-olds provide language models for the babies. Older children shout wordlessly in the excitement of a game of tag or hide-and-seek, and sometimes scold an errant toddler with a "Stop!" or "No!"—just as the Elder of Isu murmured "Hot!" when a child approached an invisible fire; though of course the Elder may have been using that circumstance as a parable, in order to make a statement of profound spiritual meaning, as appears in the Ohio Reading.

Even songs lose their words as the singers grow older. A game rhyme sung by little children has words:

> *Look at us tumbledown*
> *Stumbledown tumbledown*
> *All of us tumbledown*
> *All in a heap!*

The five- and six-year-olds pass the words of the song along to the little ones. Older children cheerfully play the games, falling into wriggling child-heaps with yells of joy, but they do not sing the words, only the tune, vocalised on a neutral syllable.

Adult Asonu often hum or sing at work, while herding, while rocking the baby. Some of the tunes are traditional, others improvised. Many employ motifs based on the whistles of the anamanu. None of the songs has words; all are hummed or vocalised. At the meetings of the clans and at marriages and funerals the ceremonial choral music is rich in melody and harmonically complex and subtle. No instruments are used, only the voice. The singers practice many days for the ceremonies. Some students of the music of the Asonu believe that their particular spiritual wisdom or insight finds its expression in these great wordless chorales.

I am inclined to agree with others who, having lived a long time among the Asonu, believe that their group singing is an element of a sacred occasion, and certainly an art, a festive communal act, and a pleasurable release of feeling, but no more. What is sacred to them remains in silence.

The little children call people by relationship words, mother, uncle, clan sister, friend, etc. If the Asonu have names, we do not know them.

About ten years ago a zealous believer in the Secret Wisdom of the Asonu kidnapped a child of four from one of the mountain clans in the dead of winter. He had obtained a zoo collector's permit, and smuggled her back to our plane in an animal cage marked anamanu. Believing that the Asonu enforce silence on their children, his plan was to encourage the little girl to keep talking as she grew up. When adult, he thought, she would thus be able to speak the innate Wisdom which her people would have obliged her to keep secret.

For the first year or so she would talk to her kidnapper, who, aside from the abominable cruelty of his action, seems to have begun by treating her kindly enough. His knowledge of the Asonu language was limited, and she saw no one else but a small group of sectarians who came to gaze worshipfully at her and listen to her talk. Her vocabulary and syntax gained no enlargement, and began to atrophy. She became increasingly silent.

Frustrated, the zealot decided to teach her English so that she would be able to express her innate Wisdom in a different tongue. We have only his report, which is that she "refused to learn," was silent or spoke almost inaudibly when he tried to make her repeat words, and "did not obey." He ceased to let other people see her. When some members of the sect finally notified the civil authorities, the child was about seven. She had spent three years hidden in a basement room. For a year or more she had been whipped and beaten regularly "to teach her to talk," her captor explained, "because she's stubborn." She was dumb, cowering, undernourished, and brutalised.

She was promptly returned to her family, who for three years had mourned her, believing she had wandered off and been lost on a glacier. They received her with tears of joy and grief. Her condition since then is not known, because the Interplanary Agency closed the entire area to all visitors, tourist or scientist, at the time she was brought back. No foreigner has been up in the Asonu mountains since. We may well imagine that her people were resentful; but nothing was ever said.

Feeling at Home with the Hennebet

I expect people who don't look like me not to be like me, a reasonable expectation, as expectations go; but it makes my mind slow to admit that people who look like me may not be like me.

The Hennebet look remarkably like me. That is to say, not only are they the same general shape and size as people on my plane, with fingers and toes and ears and all the other bits we check a baby for, but also they have pallid skin, dark hair, nearsighted eyes of mixed brown and green, and rather short, stocky figures. Their posture is terrible. The young ones are bright and agile, the old ones are thoughtful and forgetful. An unadventurous and timid people, fond of landscape and inclined to run away from strangers, they are monogamous, hardworking, slightly dyspeptic, and deeply domestic.

When I first came to their plane I felt at home at once, and—perhaps since I looked like one of them and even, in some respects, acted like one of them—the Hennebet did not show any inclination to run away from me. I stayed a week at the hostel. (The Interplanary Agency, which has existed for several kalpas, maintains hostels, inns, and luxury hotels in many popular regions, while protecting vulnerable areas from intrusion.) Then I moved to the home of a widow who supported her family by offering room and board to a few people, all of them natives but me. The widow, her two teenage children, the three other boarders, and I all ate breakfast and dinner together, and so I found myself a member of a native household. They were certainly kindly people, and Mrs. Nannattula was an excellent cook.

The Hennebet language is notoriously difficult, but I struggled along with it with the help of the translatomat provided by the Agency. I soon felt that I was beginning to know my hosts. They were not really distrustful; their shyness was mostly a defense of their privacy. When they saw I wasn't invasive, they unstiffened; and I unstiffened by making myself useful. Once I convinced Mrs. Nannattula that I really wanted to help her in the kitchen, she was happy to have a chef's apprentice. Mr. Battannele needed a listener, and I listened to him talk about politics (Hennebet is a socialist democracy run mainly by committees, not very efficiently, perhaps, but at least not disastrously). And I traded informal language lessons with Tenngo and Annup, nice adolescents. Tenngo wanted to be a biologist and her brother had a gift for languages. My translatomat was useful, but I learned most of what Hennebet I learned by teaching Annup English.

With Tenngo and Annup I seldom felt the disorientation that would come over me every now and then in conversation with the adults, a sense that I had absolutely no idea what they were talking about, that there had been an abrupt, immense discontinuity in comprehension. At first I blamed it on my poor grasp of the language, but it was more than that. There were gaps. Suddenly the Hennebet were on the other side of the gap, totally out of reach. This happened particularly often when I talked with my fellow boarder, old Mrs. Tattava. We'd start out fine, chatting about the weather or the news or her embroidery stitches, and then all at once the discontinuity would occur right in the midst of a sentence. "I find leafstitch nice for filling odd-shaped areas, but it was such a job painting the whole building with little leaves, I thought we'd never finish it!"

"What building was that?" I said.

"Hali tutuve," she said, placidly threading her needle.

I had not heard the word tutuve before. My translatomat gave it as shrine, sacred enclosure, but had nothing for hali. I went to the library and looked it up in the *Encyclopedia of Hennebet*. Hali, it said, had been a practice of the people of the Ebbo Peninsula in the previous millennium; also there was a folk dance called halihali.

Mrs. Tattava was standing halfway up the stairs with a rapt expression. I said good day. "Imagine the number of them!" she said.

"Of what?" I asked cautiously.

"The feet," she said, smiling. "One after the other, one after the other. Such a dance! So long a dance!"

After several of these excursions I asked Mrs. Nannattula in a circuitous fashion if Mrs. Tattava was having a problem with her memory. Mrs. Nannattula, chopping greens for the tunum poa, laughed and said, "Oh, she's not all there. Not at all!"

I said some conventionality—"What a pity."

My hostess glanced at me with faint puzzlement but pursued her thought, still smiling. "She says we're married! I love to talk with her. It's a real honor to have so much abba in the house, don't you think? I feel very lucky!"

I knew abba: it was a common shrub, an evergreen; we used abba berries, pungent, a bit like juniper, in certain dishes. There was an abba bush in the backyard and a little jar of the dried berries in the cupboard. But I didn't think the house was full of them.

I brooded over Mrs. Tattava's "hali shrine." I knew of no shrines at all on Hennebet, except the little niche in the living room where Mrs. Nannattula always kept a few flowers or reeds or, come to think of it, a sprig of abba. I asked her if the niche had a name, and she said it was the tutuve.

Gathering courage, I asked Mrs. Tattava, "Where is the hali tutuve?"

She did not answer for a while. "Quite far away these days," she said at last, with a faraway look. Her gaze brightened a little as it returned to me. "Were you there?"

"No."

"It's so hard to be sure," she said. "Do you know I never say I wasn't anywhere any more, because so often it turns out that I am—or are, as I should say, shouldn't we? It was very beautiful. Oh, that was so far away! And all along it's right here now!" She looked at me with such cheer and pleasure that I could not help smiling and feeling happy, though I had not the faintest idea what she was talking about.

Indeed I had at last begun to notice that the people of "my" household, and the Hennebet in general, were very much less like me than I had assumed. It was a matter of temperament, of temper. They were temperate. They were well-tempered. They were good-tempered. It was not a virtue, an ethical triumph; they simply were good-natured people. Very different from me.

Mr. Battannele talked politics with gusto and energy, with a lively interest in the problems, but it seemed to me that there was something missing, some element I was used to considering part of political talk. He didn't shift about as some weak-minded folk do, adapting his views to his interlocutor's, but he never seemed to defend any particular view of his own. Everything was left open. He would have been the most dismal failure on a radio call-in talk show or a TV experts roundtable. He lacked moral outrage. He seemed to have no convictions. Did he even have opinions?

I often went with him to the corner grogshop and listened to him discussing issues of policy with his friends, several of whom served on governing committees. All of them listened, considered, spoke, often with animation and excitement, interrupting one another to make their points; they got quite passionate; but they never got angry. Nobody ever contradicted anybody, even in such subtle ways as meeting an assertion with silence. Yet they didn't seem to be trying to avoid dissension, or to conform their

ideas to a norm, or to work towards a consensus. And most puzzling of all, these political discussions would suddenly dissolve
into laughter—chuckles, belly laughs, sometimes the whole
group ending up gasping and wiping their eyes—as if discussing
how to run the country was the same thing as sitting around
telling funny stories. I never could get the joke.

Listening on the networks, I never once heard a committee
member state that anything must be done. And yet the Hennebet
government did get things done. The country seemed to run
quite smoothly, taxes were collected, garbage was collected, pot-
holes were repaved, nobody went hungry. Elections were held at
frequent intervals; local votes on this and that issue were always
being announced on the networks, with informative material
supplied. Mrs. Nannattula and Mr. Battannele always voted.
The children often voted. When I realised that some people had
more votes than others, I was shocked.

Annup told me that Mrs. Tattava had eighteen votes, although she usually didn't bother to cast any, and probably could
have thirty or forty, if she'd bother to register.

"But why does she have more votes than other people?"

"Well, she's old, you know," the boy said. He was touch-
ingly modest when he gave me information or corrected my mis-
understandings. They all were. They acted as if they were
reminding me of something I knew that had slipped my mind.
He tried to explain: "Like, you know, I only have one vote."

"So as you get older . . . you're supposed to be wiser?"

He looked uncertain.

"Or they honor the elderly by giving them more votes . . . ?"

"Well, you already have them, you know," Annup said.

"They come back to you, you know? Or you come back to them, actually, Mother says. If you can keep them in mind. The other votes you had." I must have looked blank as a brick wall. "When you, you know, were living again." He did not say living before, he said living again.

"People remember other—their other—lives," I said, and looked for confirmation.

Annup thought it over. "I guess so," he said, uncertain. "Is that how you do it?"

"No," I said. "I mean, I never did. I don't understand."

I brought up the English word *transmigration* on my translatomat. The Hennebet translation was about birds who fly north in the rainy season and south in the dry season. I brought up *reincarnation,* and it told me about digestive processes. I brought up my big gun: *metempsychosis.* The machine told me that there was no word for this "belief" held by many peoples of the other planes that "souls" moved at death into different "bodies." The translatomat was working in Hennebet, of course, but the words I have put in quotation marks were all in English.

Annup came by while I was engaged in this research. The Hennebet use no large machinery, doing all their digging and building with hand tools, but they long ago borrowed electronic technologies from people on other planes, using them for information storage and communication and voting and so on. Annup adored the translatomat, which was to him a toy, a game. He laughed now. "'Belief'—that's thinking so?" he asked. I nodded. "What's 'souls'?" he asked.

I began with the body; it's always so much easier, you can

make gestures. "This, here, me—arms legs head stomach—body. In your language I think it's atto?"

His turn to nod.

"And your soul is in your body."

"Such as tripe?"

I tried a different tack: "If someone is dead, we say their soul is gone."

"Gone?" he echoed. "Where?"

"The body, the atto stays here—the soul goes away. Some say to an afterlife."

He stared, mystified. We spent nearly an hour on the soul-body question, trying to find some common ground in both languages and getting only more confused. The boy was unable to make any distinction at all between matter and spirit. Atto was all one was; one was all atto; how could one be anything else? There was no room for anything else. "How can there be anything more than unnua?" he finally asked me.

"So each of you—each person—is the universe?" I asked, after checking that unnua did mean universe, all, everything, all time, eternity, entirety, the whole, and finding that it also meant all the courses of a dinner, the contents of a full jug or bottle, and an infant of any species at the moment of birth.

"How could we not be? Except for slippage, of course."

At this point I had to go help his mother make dinner, and was glad to. Metaphysics was never my strong point. It was interesting that these people, who as far as I knew had no organised religion, had a metaphysics which was completely clear to a boy of fifteen. I wondered how and when he had learned it; presumably at school.

When I asked him where he had learned about atto being un-nua and so on, he disclaimed all knowledge. "I know nothing," he said. "What abba can I have? Please, talk to people who know who they are, like Mrs. Tattava!"

So I did. I plunged in. She was doing flowers in chain stitch in yellow silk by the window overlooking the canal, where she had the afternoon light. I sat down nearby and said after a while, "Mrs. Tattava, do you remember lives you lived before?"

"How could a person live more than one life?" she inquired.

"Well, why do you have eighteen votes?"

She smiled. She had an extraordinarily sweet, placid smile. "Oh, well, you know, there are all the other persons who are living this life. They're here too. Everybody gets to vote, don't they? If they want to. I'm awfully lazy. I don't like to bother with all that information. So mostly I don't vote. Do you?"

"I'm not a—" I said, and stopped, and brought up the word *citizen* on my translatomat. It said that the Hennebet word for citizen was person.

"I am not sure who I am," I said cautiously.

"Many people never are," she said, quite earnestly now, looking up from her chain stitch. Her eyes amidst their wrinkles and behind their bifocals were brownish-green. The Hennebet seldom look directly at one, but she gazed at me. The gaze was kind, serene, remote, and brief. I felt that she did not see me very clearly. "But it doesn't matter, you know," she said. "If for one moment of your whole life you know that you are, then that's your life, that moment, that's unnua, that's all. In a short life I saw my mother's face, like the sun, so I'm here. In a long life I went there and there and there; but I dug in the garden, the root of a weed came up in my hand, so I'm unnua. When you get old, you know, you keep being here instead of there, everything is here. Everything is here," she repeated, with a comfortable little laugh, and went on with her embroidery.

I have talked to other people about the Hennebet. Some of them are convinced that the Hennebet do literally experience reincarnation, remembering more and more of their previous lives as they grow older, until at death they rejoin an innumerable multitude of former selves, and are then reborn bringing this immaterial trail or train of old lives into a new life.

But I can't square this with the fact that soul and body are a single thing to them, so that either nothing or everything is material or immaterial. Nor does it fit with what Mrs. Tattava said about "all the other persons living this life." She did not say "other lives." She did not say "living this life at other times." She said, "They're here too."

I have no idea what abba is, aside from the plant with pungent little berries.

All I can really say about the Hennebet is that a few months with them confused my expectations of identity and my ideas about time very much, and that since my visit to them I seem unable to maintain a really strong opinion about anything; but that is neither here nor there.

The Ire of the Veksi

Not many people visit the Veksian plane. They are afraid its
inhabitants will hurt them. In fact, the Veksi resolutely ignore visitors from other planes, considering them to be the impotent and evil-smelling ghosts of dead enemies who will go
away if no attention at all is paid to them. This has generally
proved to be true.

Some students of the varieties of behavior have, however,
stayed and learned a good deal about their unwilling and indifferent hosts. The following description was given to me by a
friend who wishes to remain anonymous.

The Veksi are an angry species. Their social life consists
largely of arguments, recriminations, quarrels, fights, outbursts

of fury, fits of the sulks, brawls, feuds, and impulsive acts of vengeance.

There is no difference in size or strength between the men and the women of the Veksi. Both sexes supplement their natural strength with weapons, carried at all times. Their mating is often so violent that it causes injury and occasionally death to one or both of the participants.

They go about mostly on all fours, though they can and do walk upright with vigorous grace on their short, strong hind limbs, which end in hoofs. The Veksi forelimb is so jointed that the limb can be used equally well as a leg or arm. The slender forehoof encloses and protects a hand, kept curled in a fist inside the hoof when it is walked upon. When extended from the hoof, the four opposable digits are as dextrous and graceful as the human hand.

The hair of the Veksi grows coarse and long on the head and back, and as a fine, thick down or fur everywhere else on the body except the palms and genitals. The skin color is tan or brown, the hair color black, brown, tan, rusty, or a mixture of these in various brindles and shadings. As the Veksi age, white hairs appear, and old Veksi may be pure white; but there are not many old Veksi.

Clothing, being unnecessary for protection from cold or heat, is a matter of belts, harnesses, and ribbons, worn as adornment and to furnish pockets and holsters for tools and weapons.

The irritability of the Veksi temperament makes it hard for them to live together, but their need for social stimulation and conflict makes it impossible for them to live apart. The common solution is a fenced village of five or six large domed clay houses and fifteen or twenty small ones, built partly underground. These houses are called omedra.

The large, many-roomed omedra contain households, usually a group of related women and their children or sexually partnered women and their children. Men—relatives, sexual partners, and friends—can join a household only on invitation, may leave at will, and must leave if ordered out by the women. If they don't leave, all the women and most of the other men attack them savagely, drive them away bleeding, and throw stones at them if they try to return.

The small, one-room omedra are occupied by single adults, called solitaries. Solitaries are men who have been driven out of the big omedra and men and women who choose to live alone. Solitaries may frequent one or more households; they work in the fields with the others, but they sleep and eat most meals alone. An early visitor described a Veksi village as "five big houses full of women swearing at each other and fourteen little houses full of men sulking."

This pattern is maintained in the cities, which are essentially villages banded together against other groups of villages, built on river islands or defensible mesas or surrounded by moats and earthworks. The cities are divided into distinct neighborhoods socially similar to the rural villages. Rancor, rivalry, and hatred prevail amongst all neighbors in villages, cities, and city neighborhoods. Feuds and forays are continuous. Most men and women die of wounds. Though war on a large scale, involving more than a few villages or two cities, seems to be unknown, peaceful coexistence of villages or neighborhoods rests on temporary and contemptuous avoidance, and is always of brief duration.

The Veksi have no value for power or control over others, and do not fight to gain dominion. They fight in anger and for revenge.

This may explain why, though Veksi intelligence and technological skill could easily have achieved weapons that kill at a distance, they fight with knife, dagger, and club, or barehanded—barehoofed. In fact their fighting is restricted by a great many unspoken traditions or customs of great authority. For example, no matter what the provocation, they never destroy crops or orchards in their raids and vendettas.

I visited a rural village, Akagrak, all of whose adult men had been killed in fights and feuds with three nearby villages. None of the rich river-bottom land of Akagrak had been harmed or taken by the victors in these battles.

I witnessed the funeral of the last man of the village, a White—that is, an old man—who had gone out alone to avenge his murdered nephew and had been stoned to death by a troop of youths from one of the other villages, Tkat. Killing by throwing stones is a transgression of the code of battle. The people of Akagrak were furious, their outrage not softened by the fact that the people of Tkat had punished their own young transgressors so severely that one died and another was lamed for life. In Akagrak the surviving males, six boys, were not allowed to go into battle till they turned fifteen, the age when all Veksi men and some women become Warriors. Along with the girls under fifteen, the boys were working very hard in the fields, trying to replace the dead men. All the Warriors of Akagrak were now women who had no children or whose children were grown.

These women spent most of their time ambushing people from Tkat and the other villages.

Women who are bringing up children are not Warriors; they fight only defensively, except when a child has been murdered. Then the mother leads the other women in a vengeance raid. The Veksi do not normally invade one another's villages and do not intentionally attack or kill children. But children of course get killed in the furious battles. A child's death is called murder and justifies invasion. The non-Warrior women, the avenging mothers, walk openly into the murderers' village. They don't kill any children, but they will kill any man or woman who fights back. Their moral advantage is such that they are seldom met with resistance. The guilty villagers simply sit in the dirt and await punishment. The avengers kick, beat, revile, and spit on them. Usually they demand a blood gift, a child to replace the murdered one. They don't kidnap or force a child to come with them. A child has to agree or volunteer to go with them. Curiously enough, this is what usually happens.

Children under fifteen also quite often run away to a neighboring, which is to say an enemy, village. There they can count on being accepted into a household. The runaways may stay till their spite against their own people is out, or even permanently. I asked such a child, a girl of about nine, in Akagrak, why she had left her village. She said, "I was mad at Ma."

In the cities, children are frequent accidental victims of the almost constant street fighting. Their death may be avenged, but their avengers are not immune, as they are in the villages, for in the cities the social code has decayed or broken down altogether.

The three large cities of the Veksi are so dangerous that people over thirty are a rare sight in their streets. Yet they are constantly repopulated by runaways from the villages.

The children of the Veksi are handled pretty roughly from infancy on. There is no doubt that Veksi parents passionately love their own and feel a strong responsibility towards all children—as witness the fact that runaways are always taken in and treated just as well (or badly) as the children of the village. Babies get constant care and attention from the parents and relatives, a fierce, impatient care, never tender. Slaps, shakes, curses, shouts, and threats are the stuff of every child's life. Adults do try to govern their fierce tempers with children under fifteen. A violent child beater will be beaten by other adults, and a solitary who hurts children will be, literally, kicked out of the village.

The children treat all adults warily. Holding their own among their peers is less of a problem. Much of their quarrelsome behavior seems to be imitative. Veksi babies are silent, watchful, and stoical. When not with adults, Veksi children work and play together quite peaceably. This behavior changes as they approach the Warrior age of fifteen, when, whether driven by physiological changes or by cultural expectations, they begin to pick fights, retaliate fiercely to any slight, and indulge in prolonged sulks that flare into fits of berserk rage.

Visiting a large omedra full of wrathful people, one gets the impression that adult Veksi do nothing but shout, scold, swear, and quarrel, but the real rule of their life is avoidance. Most adults even in a household, certainly the solitaries, spend most of the time belligerently maintaining distance and independence.

This is one reason they find it so easy to ignore us "ghosts"—they ignore one another most of the time. It's unwise for a Veksi ever to come closer than arm's length to another Veksi without a clear invitation. It's dangerous for anybody, sister or stranger, to approach a solitary's house. If they have to do so, they stand at a distance and shout various ritual statements of warning and appeasement. Even so the solitary may ignore them, or come out with a scowl and a short sword to run them off. Women solitaries are notoriously even more short-tempered and dangerous than the men.

Despite their irritability with one another, the Veksi can and do work together. Most of their highly effective agriculture is communal, pursued according to efficient and unvarying custom. Fierce arguments and quarrels arise unceasingly over details of the customs, but the work goes on.

The tubers and grains they raise are rich in protein and carbohydrates; they eat no meat except for several kinds of grub, the larvae of insects encouraged to live on their crops, which they use for flavoring and condiments. They brew a strong beer from one of their seed crops.

Except for parents restraining or directing their children (often in the face of sullen or screaming resistance), no person claims authority over another. There are no chiefs in the villages, no bosses in the fields or the city factories. There is no social hierarchy.

They do not accumulate wealth, avoiding economic dominance as they avoid social dominance. Anyone who gains possessions much exceeding those of the rest of the community promptly gives everything away or spends it on community needs, such as building repairs, tools, or weapons. Men often give weapons to people they hate, either as a shaming device or as a kind of dare. Women, being in charge of the households, the young, and the infirm, have the right to hoard food against bad times; but if a household has a bumper crop, they share it out as fast as possible, giving grain away, and putting on lavish feasts for the whole village. Much beer is drunk at these feasts. I expected that drinking would lead the Veksi straight to carnage, and was quite alarmed the first time I found myself observing a village feast; but beer seems to mellow the Veksi rage, and instead of quarreling with each other they're likely to spend the night getting sentimental over old deaths and quarrels, weeping together and showing each other their scars.

The Veksi are rigid monotheists. Their god is conceived as the force of destruction, against which no creature can long stand. To them, existence is a rebellion against law. Human life is a brief defiance of inevitable doom. The stars themselves are mere sparks in the fire of annihilation. Names of God in various Veksi rituals and chants are: Ender, Vast Devastator, Ineluctable Hoof, Waiting Void, Rock That Smashes Brain.

Images of the deity are black stones, some natural, some carved and polished into globes or disks. Private or community worship consists mainly of lighting a fire before one of these stones and chanting or shouting ritual words and verses. Wooden drums are kicked furiously with the rear hoofs, making a terrible noise. There is no priesthood, but adults make sure the children learn the ceremonies.

I was present at the funeral of the White man of Akagrak. His body was laid out on a plank, unclothed; the sacred stone of his omedra was laid on his chest, and a black pebble was placed in each of his hands, curled within his forehoofs. Four of his closest relatives carried the body to the burning ground, walking upright. All the people of the village followed on all fours. A big pyre of logs and brushwood was ready, and the corpse was set atop it. Nearby a smaller fire of knots had been smoldering for an hour or so. People picked up burning knots and embers with their bare hands and hurled them into the pyre, shouting and screaming in what appeared to be pure, uncontrolled rage. The dead man's granddaughter yelled over and over, "How could you do this to me? How could you go and die? You didn't really love me! I'll never forgive you!" Other relatives and descendants ranted at the dead man for not caring that they loved him, for abandoning them, running away when they needed him, living so long and then dying after all. Many of these accusations and up-braidings were clearly ritual and traditional, but they were delivered with unmistakable anger. People wept, tore off their belts and ornaments and hurled them cursing into the fire, tore at the hair of their head and arms, rubbed dirt and soot on their faces and bodies. Whenever the fire began to burn low they ran for more fuel and piled it on furiously. Children who cried were impatiently given a handful of dried fruit and told, "Shut up! Eat your teeth! Grandfather is not listening! Grandfather has deserted you! You are worthless orphans now!"

As evening came on, the pyre at last was allowed to burn down. The body had been entirely consumed. There was no burial of what bone fragments may have been left in the ashes and embers, but the sacred black stone was retrieved and restored to its shrine. The people, exhausted, dragged themselves back to the village, locked the gates for the night, and went to bed fasting and unwashed, with burned hands and sore hearts. There was no doubt in my mind that all the villagers had been proud of the old man, for it is a real achievement for a Veksi to live to be a White, and that some of them had loved him dearly; but their laments were accusations, their grief was rage.

Seasons of the Ansarac

To the Ospreys of McKenzie Bridge, whose lifestyle inspired this story

I talked for a long time once with an old Ansar. I met him at his Interplanary Hostel, which is on a large island far out in the Great Western Ocean, well away from the migratory routes of the Ansarac. It is the only place visitors from other planes are allowed, these days.

Kergemmeg lives there as a native host and guide, to give visitors a little whiff of local color, for otherwise the place is like a tropical island on any of a hundred planes—sunny, breezy, lazy, beautiful, with feathery trees and golden sands and great, blue-green, white-maned waves breaking on the reef out past the lagoon. Most visitors come to sail, fish, beachcomb, and drink fermented ü, and have no interest otherwise in the plane or in the sole native of it they have met. They look at him, at first, and take photos, of course, for he is a striking figure: about seven feet tall, thin, strong, angular, a little stooped by age, with a narrow head, large, round, black-and-gold eyes, and a beak. There is an all-or-nothing quality about a beak that keeps the beaked face from being as expressive as those on which the nose and mouth are separated, but Kergemmeg's eyes and eyebrows reveal his feelings very clearly. Old he may be, but he is a passionate man.

He was a little bored and lonely among the uninterested tourists, and when he found me a willing listener (surely not the first or last, but currently the only one), he took pleasure in telling me about his people, as we sat with a tall glass of iced ü in the long, soft evenings, in a purple darkness all aglow with the light of the stars, the shining of the sea waves full of luminous creatures, and the pulsing glimmer of clouds of fireflies up in the fronds of the feather trees.

From time immemorial, he said, the Ansarac have followed a Way. *Madan*, he called it. The way of my people, the way things are done, the way things are, the way to go, the way that is hidden in the word *always*: like ours, his word held all those meanings. "Then we strayed from our Way," he said. "For a little while. Now again we do as we have always done."

People are always telling you that "we have always done thus," and then you find that their "always" means a generation or two, or a century or two, at most a millennium or two. Cultural ways and habits are blips compared to the ways and habits of the body, of the race. There really is very little that human beings on our plane have always done, except find food and drink, sleep, sing, talk, procreate, nurture the children, and probably band together to some extent. Indeed it can be seen as our human essence, how few behavioral imperatives we follow. How flexible we are in finding new things to do, new ways to go. How ingeniously, inventively, desperately we seek the right way, the true way, the Way we believe we lost long ago among the thickets of novelty and opportunity and choice . . .

The Ansarac had a somewhat different choice to make than we did, perhaps a more limited one. But it has its interest.

Their world has a larger sun than ours and is farther from it, so, though its spin and tilt are much the same as Earth's, its year lasts about twenty-four of ours. And the seasons are correspondingly large and leisurely, each of them six of our years long.

On every plane and in every climate that has a spring, spring is the breeding time, when new life is born; and for creatures whose life is only a few seasons or a few years, early spring is mating time, too, when new life begins. So it is for the Ansarac, whose life span is, in their terms, three years.

They inhabit two continents, one on the equator and a little north of it, one that stretches up towards the north pole; the two are joined by a long, mountainous bridge of land, as the Americas are, though it is all on a smaller scale. The rest of the world is ocean, with a few archipelagoes and scattered large islands, none with any human population except the one used by the Interplanary Agency.

The year begins, Kergemmeg said, when in the cities of the

plains and deserts of the south, the Year Priests give the word and great crowds gather to see the sun pause at the peak of a certain tower or stab through a certain target with an arrow of light at dawn: the moment of solstice. Now increasing heat will parch the southern grasslands and prairies of wild grain, and in the long dry season the rivers will run low and the wells of the city will go dry. Spring follows the sun northward, melting snow from those far hills, brightening valleys with green...And the Ansarac will follow the sun.

"Well, I'm off," old friend says to old friend in the city street. "See you around!" And the young people, the almost-one-year-olds—to us they'd be people of twenty-one or twenty-two—drift away from their households and groups of pals, their colleges and sports clubs, and seek out, among the labyrinthine apartment complexes and communal dwellings and hostelries of the city, one or the other of the parents from whom they parted, back in the summer. Sauntering casually in, they remark, "Hullo, Dad," or "Hullo, Mother. Seems like everybody's going back north." And the parent, careful not to insult by offering guidance over the long route they came half the young one's life ago, says, "Yes, I've been thinking about it myself. It certainly would be nice to have you with us. Your sister's in the other room, packing."

And so by ones, twos, and threes, the people abandon the city. The exodus is a long process, without any order to it. Some people leave quite soon after the solstice, and others say about them, "What a hurry they're in," or, "Shennenne just has to get there first so she can grab the old homesite." Some people linger in the city till it is almost empty, and still can't make up their mind to leave the hot and silent streets, the sad, shadeless, deserted squares that were so full of crowds and music all through the long half year. But first and last they all set out on the roads that lead north. And once they go, they go with speed.

Most carry with them only what they can carry in a backpack or load on a ruba (from Kergemmeg's description, rubac are something like small, feathered donkeys). Some of the traders who have become wealthy during the desert season start out with whole trains of rubac loaded with goods and treasures. Though most people travel alone or in a small family group, on the more popular roads they follow pretty close after one another. Larger groups form temporarily in places where the going is hard and the older and weaker people need help gathering and carrying food.

There are no children on the road north.

Kergemmeg did not know how many Ansarac there are but guessed some hundreds of thousands, perhaps a million. All of them join the migration.

As they go up into the mountainous Middle Lands, they do not bunch together, but spread out onto hundreds of different tracks, some taken by many, others by only a few, some clearly marked, others so cryptic that only people who have been on them before could ever trace the turnings. "That's when it's good to have a three-year-old along," Kergemmeg said. "Somebody who's been up the way twice." They travel very light and very fast. They live off the land except in the arid heights of the mountains, where, as he said, "They lighten their packs." And up in those passes and high canyons, the hard-driven rubac of the traders' caravans begin to stumble and tremble, perishing of exhaustion and cold. If a trader still tries to drive them on, people on the road unload them and loose them and let their own pack beast go with them. The little animals limp and scramble southward, back down to the desert. The goods they carried end up strewn along the wayside for anyone to take; but nobody takes anything, except a little food at need. They don't want stuff to carry, to slow them down. Spring is coming, cool spring, sweet spring, to the valleys of grass and the forests, the lakes, the bright rivers of the north, and they want to be there when it comes.

Listening to Kergemmeg, I imagined that if one could see the migration from above, see those people all threading along a thousand paths and trails, it would be like watching our northwest coast in spring a century or two ago when every stream, from the mile-wide Columbia to the tiniest creek, turned red with the salmon run.

The salmon spawn and die when they reach their goal, and some of the Ansarac are going home to die, too: those on their third migration north, the three-year-olds, whom we would see as people of seventy and over. Some of them don't make it all the way. Worn out by privation and hard going, they drop behind. If people pass an old man or woman sitting by the road, they may speak a word or two, help to put up a little shelter, leave a gift of food, but they do not urge the elder to come with them. If the elder is very weak or ill they may wait a night or two, until perhaps another migrant takes their place. If they find an old person dead by the roadside, they bury the body. On its back, with the feet to the north: going home.

There are many, many graves along the roads north, Kergemmeg said. Nobody has ever made a fourth migration.

The younger people, those on their first and second migrations, hurry on, crowded together in the high passes of the mountains, then spreading out ever wider on a myriad of paths through the prairies as the Middle Lands widen out north of the mountains. By the time they reach the northland proper, the great rivers of people have tasseled out into thousands of rivulets, veering west and east, across the north.

Coming to a pleasant hill country where the grass is already green and the trees are leafing, one of the little groups comes to a halt. "Well, here we are," says Mother. "Here it is." There are tears in her eyes and she laughs the soft, clacking laugh of the Ansarac. "Shuku, do you remember this place?"

And the daughter who was less than a half year old when she left this place—eleven or so, in our years—stares around with amazement and incredulity, and laughs, and cries, "But it was *bigger* than this!"

Then perhaps Shuku looks across those half-familiar meadows of her birthplace to the just visible roof of the nearest neighbor and wonders if Kimimmid and his father, who caught up to them and camped with them for a few nights and then went on ahead, were there already, living there, and if so, would Kimimmid come over to say hello?

For the people who lived so close-packed, in such sociable and ceaseless promiscuity in the Cities under the Sun, sharing rooms, sharing beds, sharing work and play, doing everything together in groups and crowds, now have all gone apart, family from family, friend from friend, each to a small and separate house here in the meadowlands, or farther north in the rolling hills, or still farther north in the lakelands. But if they have all scattered like sand from a broken hourglass, the bonds that unite them have not broken, only changed. Now they come together not in groups and crowds, not in tens and hundreds and thousands, but by two and two.

"Well, here you are!" says Shuku's mother, as Shuku's father opens the door of the little house at the meadow's edge. "You must have been just a few days ahead of us."

"Welcome home," he says gravely. His eyes shine. The two adults take each other by the hand and slightly raise their narrow, beaked heads in a particular salute, an intimate yet formal greeting. Shuku suddenly remembers seeing them do that when she was a little girl, when they lived here, long ago. Here at the birthplace.

"Kimimmid was asking about you just yesterday," Father says to Shuku, and he softly clacks a laugh.

Spring is coming, spring is upon them. Now they will perform the ceremonies of the spring.

Kimimmid comes across the meadow to visit, and he and Shuku talk together, and walk together in the meadows and down by the stream. Presently, after a day or a week or two, he asks her if she would like to dance. "Oh, I don't know," she says, but seeing him stand tall and straight, his head thrown back a little, in the posture that begins the dance, she too stands up; at first her head is lowered, though she stands straight, arms at her sides; but then she wants to throw her head back, back, to reach her arms out wide, wide...to dance, to dance with him...

And what are Shuku's parents and Kimimmid's parents doing, in the kitchen garden or out in the old orchard, but the same thing? They face each other, they raise their proud and narrow heads, and then the man leaps, arms raised above his head, a great leap and a bow, a low bow...and the woman bows too... And so it goes, the courtship dance. All over the northern continent, now, the people are dancing.

Nobody interferes with the older couples, recourting, refashioning their marriage. But Kimimmid had better look out. A young man comes across the meadow one evening, a young man Shuku never met before; his birthplace is some miles away. He has heard of Shuku's beauty. He sits and talks with her. He tells her that he is building a new house, in a grove of trees, a pretty spot, nearer her home than his. He would like her advice on how to build the house. He would like very much to dance with her sometime. Maybe this evening, just for a little, just a step or two, before he goes away?

He is a wonderful dancer. Dancing with him on the grass in the late evening of early spring, Shuku feels that she is flying on a great wind, and she closes her eyes, her hands float out from her sides as if on that wind, and meet his hands...

Her parents will live together in the house by the meadow; they will have no more children, for that time is over for them, but they will make love as often as ever they did when they first were married. Shuku will choose one of her suitors, the new one, in fact. She goes to live with him and make love with him in the house they finish building together. Their building, their dancing, gardening, eating, sleeping, everything they do, turns into making love. And in due course Shuku is pregnant; and in due course she bears two babies. Each is born in a tough, white membrane or shell. Both parents tear this protective covering open with hands and beaks, freeing the tiny curled-up newborn, who lifts its infinitesimal beaklet and peeps blindly, already gaping, greedy for food, for life.

The second baby, smaller, is not greedy, does not thrive. Though Shuku and her husband both feed her with tender care, and though Shuku's mother comes to stay and feeds the little one from her own beak and rocks her endlessly when she cries, still she pines and weakens. One morning lying in her grandmother's arms the infant twists and gasps for breath, and then is still. The grandmother weeps bitterly, remembering Shuku's baby brother, who did not live even this long, and tries to comfort Shuku. The baby's father digs a small grave out back of the new house, among the budding trees of the long springtime, and the tears fall from his eyes as he digs. But the other baby, the big girl, Kikirri, chirps and clacks and eats and thrives.

About the time Kikirri is hauling herself upright and shouting "Da!" at her father and "Ma!" at her mother and grandmother and "No!" when told to stop what she is doing, Shuku has another baby. Like many second conceptions, it is a singleton. A fine boy, small, but greedy. He grows fast.

He will be the last of Shuku's children. She and her husband will make love still, whenever they please, in all the delight and ease of the time of flowering and the time of fruit, in the warm days and the mild nights, in the cool under the trees and out in the buzzing heat of the meadow in summer noontime, but it will be, as they say, luxury love; nothing will come of it but love itself.

Children are born to the Ansarac only in the early northern spring, soon after they have returned to their birthplace. Some couples bring up four children, and many three; but often, if the first two thrive, there is no second conception.

"You are spared our curse of overbreeding," I said to Kergemmeg when he had told me all this. And he agreed, when I told him a little about my plane.

But he did not want me to think that an Ansar has no sexual or reproductive choice at all. Pair bonding is the rule, but human will and contrariness change and bend and break it, and he talked about those exceptions. Many pair bonds are between two men or two women. Such couples and others who are childless are often given a baby by a couple who have three or four, or take on an orphaned child and bring it up. There are people who take no mate and people who take several mates at one time or in sequence. There is of course adultery. And there is rape. It is bad to be a girl among the last migrants coming up from the south, for the sexual drive is already strong in such stragglers, and young women are all too often gang-raped and arrive at their birthplace brutalised, mateless, and pregnant. A man who finds no mate or is dissatisfied with his wife may leave home and go off as a peddler of needles and thread or as a tool sharpener and tinker; such wanderers are welcomed for their goods but mistrusted as to their motives.

When we had talked together through several of those glimmering purple evenings on the veranda in the soft sea breeze, I asked Kergemmeg about his own life. He had followed Madan, the rule, the Way, in all respects but one, he said. He mated after his first migration north. His wife bore two children, both from the first conception, a girl and a boy, who of course went south with them in due time. The whole family rejoined for his second migration north, and both children had married close by, so that he knew his five grandchildren well. He and his wife had spent most of their third season in the south in different cities; she, a teacher of astronomy, had gone farther south to the Observatory, while he stayed in Terke Keter to study with a group of philosophers. She died very suddenly of a heart attack. He attended her funeral. Soon after that he made the trek back north with his son and grandchildren. "I didn't miss her till I came back home," he said, factually. "But to come there to our house, to live there without her—that wasn't something I could do. I happened to hear that someone was needed to greet the strangers on this island. I had been thinking about the best way to die, and this seemed a sort of halfway point. An island in the middle of the ocean, with not another soul of my people on it...not quite life, not quite death. The idea amused me. So I am here." He was well over three Ansar years old; getting on for eighty in our years, though only the slight stoop of his shoulders and the pure silver of his crest showed his age.

The next night he told me about the southern migration, describing how a man of the Ansarac feels as the warm days of the northern summer begin to wane and shorten. All the work of harvest is done, the grain stored in airtight bins for next year, the slow-growing edible roots planted to winter through and be ready in the spring; the children are shooting up tall, active, increasingly restless and bored by life on the homeplace, more and more inclined to wander off and make friends with the neighbors' children. Life is sweet here but the same, always the same, and luxury love has lost its urgency. One night, a cloudy night with a chill in the air, your wife in bed next to you sighs and murmurs, "You know? I miss the city." And it comes back to you in a great wave of light and warmth—the crowds, the deep streets and high houses packed with people, the Year Tower high above it all—the sports arenas blazing with sunlight, the squares at night full of lantern lights and music where you sit at the café tables and drink ü and talk and talk halfway to morning—the old friends, friends you haven't thought of all this time—and strangers—how long has it been since you saw a new face? How long since you heard a new idea, had a new thought? Time for the city, time to follow the sun!

"Dear," the mother says, "we can't take *all* your rock collection south, just pick out the most special ones," and the child protests, "But I'll *carry* them! I promise!" Forced at last to yield, she finds a special, secret place for her rocks till she comes back, never imagining that by next year, when she comes back home, she won't care about her childish rock collection, and scarcely aware that she has begun to think constantly of the great journey and the unknown lands ahead. The city! What do you do in the city? Are there rock collections?

"Yes," Father says. "In the museum. Very fine collections. They'll take you to see all the museums when you're in school."

School?

"You'll love it," Mother says with absolute certainty.

"School is the best good time in the world," says Aunt Kekki. "I loved school so much, I think I'm going to teach school, this year."

The migration south is quite a different matter from the migration north. It is not a scattering but a grouping, a gathering. It is not haphazard but orderly, planned by all the families of a region for many days beforehand. They set off together, five or ten or fifteen families, and camp together at night. They bring plenty of food with them in handcarts and barrows, cooking utensils, fuel for fires in the treeless plains, warm clothing for the mountain passes, and medicines for illness along the way.

There are no old people on the southward migration—nobody over seventy or so in our years. Those who have made three migrations stay behind. They group together in farmsteads or the small towns that have grown around the farmsteads, or they live out the end of their life with their mate, or alone, in the house where they lived the springs and summers of their lives. (I think what Kergemmeg meant, when he said he had followed his people's Way in all ways but one, was that he had not stayed home but had come to the island.) The "winter parting," as it is called, between the young going south and the old staying home is painful. It is stoical. It is as it must be.

Only those who stay behind will ever see the glory of autumn in the northern lands, the blue length of dusk, the first faint patterns of ice on the lake. Some have made paintings or left letters describing these things for the children and grandchildren they will not see again. Most die before the long, long darkness and cold of winter. None survive it.

Each migrating group, as it comes down towards the Middle Lands, is joined by others coming from east and west, till at night the twinkle of campfires covers the great prairie from horizon to horizon. The people sing at the campfires, and the quiet singing hovers in the darkness between the little fires and the stars.

They don't hurry on the southward journey. They drift along

easily, not far each day, though they keep moving. As they reach the foothills of the mountains, the great masses split again onto many different paths, thinning out, for it's pleasanter to be few on a trail than to come after great numbers of people and trudge in the dust and litter they leave. Up in the heights and passes where there are only a few ways to go, they have to come together again. They make the best of it, with cheerful greetings and offers to share food, fire, shelter. Everyone is kind to the children, the half-year-olds, who find the steep mountain paths hard going and often frightening; they slow their pace for the children.

And one evening when it seems they have been struggling in the mountains forever, they come through a high, stony pass to the outlook—South Face, or the Godsbeak Rocks, or the Tor. There they stand and look out and out and down and down to the golden, sunlit levels of the south, the endless fields of wild grain, and some far, faint, purple smudges—the walls and towers of the Cities under the Sun.

On the downhill road they go faster, and eat lighter, and the dust of their going is a great cloud behind them.

They come to the cities—there are nine of them; Terke Keter is the largest—standing full of sand and silence and sunlight. They pour in through the gates and doors, they fill the streets, they light the lanterns, they draw water from the brimming wells, they throw their bedding down in empty rooms, they shout from window to window and from roof to roof.

Life in the cities is so different from life in the homesteads that the children can't believe it; they are disturbed and dubious; they disapprove. It is so noisy, they complain. It's hot. There isn't anywhere to be alone, they say. They weep, the first nights, from homesickness. But they go off to school as soon as the schools are organised, and there they meet everybody else their age, all of them disturbed and dubious and disapproving and shy and eager and wild with excitement. Back home, they all learned to read and write and do arithmetic, just as they learned carpentry and farming, taught by their parents; but here are advanced classes, libraries, museums, galleries of art, concerts of music, teachers of art, of literature, of mathematics, of astronomy, of architecture, of philosophy—here are sports of all kinds, games, gymnastics, and somewhere in the city every night there is a round dance—above all, here is everybody else in the world, all crowded into these yellow walls, all meeting and talking and working and thinking together in an endless ferment of mind and occupation.

The parents seldom stay together in the cities. Life there is not lived by twos but in groups. They drift apart, following friends, pursuits, professions, and see each other now and then. The children stay at first with one parent or the other, but after a while they too want to be on their own and go off to live in one of the warrens of young people, the communal houses, the dormitories of the colleges. Young men and women live together, as do grown men and women. Gender is not of much import where there is no sexuality.

For they do everything under the sun in the Cities under the Sun, except make love.

They love, they hate, they learn, they make, they think hard, work hard, play; they enjoy passionately and suffer desperately, they live a full and human life, and they never give a thought to sex—unless, as Kergemmeg said with a perfect poker face, they are philosophers.

Their achievements, their monuments as a people, are all in the Cities under the Sun, whose towers and public buildings, as I saw in a book of drawings Kergemmeg showed me, vary from stern purity to fervent magnificence. Their books are written there, their thought and religion took form there over the centuries. Their history, their continuity as a culture, is all there.

Their continuity as living beings is what they see to in the north.

Kergemmeg said that while they are in the south they do not miss their sexuality at all. I had to take him at his word, which was given, hard as it might be for us to imagine, simply as a statement of fact.

And as I try to tell here what he told me, it seems wrong to describe their life in the cities as celibate or chaste: for those words imply a forced or willed resistance to desire. Where there is no desire there is no resistance, no abstinence, but rather what one might call, in a radical sense of the word, innocence. Their marital life is an empty memory to them, meaningless. If a couple stays together or meets often in the south it is because they are uncommonly good friends—because they love each other. But they love their other friends too. They never live separately from other people. There is little privacy in the great apartment houses of the cities—nobody cares about it. Life there is communal, active, sociable, gregarious, and full of pleasures.

But slowly the days grow warmer, the air drier; there is a restlessness in the air. The shadows begin to fall differently. And the crowds gather in the streets to hear the Year Priests announce the solstice and watch the sun stop, and pause, and turn south.

People leave the cities, one here, a couple there, a family there . . . It has begun to stir again, that soft hormonal buzz in the blood, that first vague yearning intimation or memory, the body's knowledge of its kingdom coming.

The young people follow that knowledge blindly, without knowing they know it. The married couples are drawn back together by all their wakened memories, intensely sweet. To go home, to go home and be there together!

All they learned and did all those thousands of days and nights in the cities is left behind them, packed up, put away. Till they come back south again . . .

"That is why it was easy to turn us aside," Kergemmeg said. "Because our lives in the north and the south are so different that they seem, to you others, incoherent, incomplete. And we cannot connect them rationally. We cannot explain or justify our Madan to those who live only one kind of life. When the Bayderac came to our plane, they told us our Way was mere instinct and that we lived like animals. We were ashamed."

(I later checked Kergemmeg's "Bayderac" in the *Encyclopedia Planaria,* where I found an entry for the Beidr, of the Unon Plane, an aggressive and enterprising people with highly advanced material technologies, who have been in trouble more than once with the Interplanary Agency for interfering on other planes. The tourist guidebook gives them the symbols that mean "of special interest to engineers, computer programmers, and systems analysts.")

Kergemmeg spoke of them with a kind of pain. It changed his voice, tightened it. He had been a child when they arrived—

the first visitors, as it happened, from another plane. He had thought about them the rest of his life.

"They told us we should take control of our lives. We should not live two separate half lives but live fully all the time, all the year, as all intelligent beings do. They were a great people, full of knowledge, with high sciences and great ease and luxury of life. To them we truly were little more than animals. They told us and showed us how other people lived on other planes. We saw we were foolish to do without the pleasure of sex for half our life. We saw we were foolish to spend so much time and energy going between south and north on foot, when we could make ships, or roads and cars, or airplanes, and go back and forth a hundred times a year if we liked. We saw we could build cities in the north and make homesteads in the south. Why not? Our Madan was wasteful and irrational, a mere animal impulse controlling us. All we had to do to be free of it was take the medicines the Bayderac gave us. And our children need not take medicines, but could have their being altered by the genetic science of Bayder. Then we could be without rest from sexual desire until we got very old, like the Bayderac. And then a woman would be able to get pregnant at any time before her menopause—in the south, even. And the number of her children would not be limited... They were eager to give us these medicines. We knew their doctors were wise. As soon as they came to us, they had given us treatments for some of our illnesses that cured people as if by a miracle. They knew so much. We saw them fly about in their airplanes, and envied them, and were ashamed.

"They brought machines for us. We tried to drive the cars

they gave us on our narrow, rocky roads. They sent engineers to direct us, and we began to build a huge highway straight through the Middle Lands. We blew up mountains with the explosives the Bayderac gave us so the highway could run wide and level, south to north and north to south. My father was a workman on the highway. There were thousands of men working on that road, for a while. Men from the southern homesteads... Only men. Women were not asked to go and do that work. Bayder women did not do such work. Women were to stay home with the children, they told us, while men did the work."

Kergemmeg sipped his ü thoughtfully and gazed off at the glimmering sea and the star-dusted sky.

"Women went down from the homesteads and talked to the men," he said. "They said to listen to them, not only to the Bayderac...Perhaps women don't feel shame the way men do. Perhaps their shame is different, more a matter of the body than the mind. They didn't care much for the cars and airplanes and bulldozers but cared a great deal about the medicines that would change us and the rules about who did which kind of work. After all, with us, the woman bears the child, but both parents feed it, both nurture it. Why should a child be left to the mother only? They asked that. How could a woman alone bring up four children? Or more than four children? It was inhuman. And then, in the cities, why should families stay together? The child doesn't want its parents then, the parents don't want the child, they all have other things to do...The women talked about this to us men, and with them we tried to talk about it to the Bayderac.

"They said, 'All that will change. You will see. You cannot reason correctly. It is merely an effect of your hormones, your genetic programming, which we will correct. Then you will be free of your irrational and useless behavior patterns.'

"We answered, 'But will we be free of *your* irrational and useless behavior patterns?'

"Men working on the highway began throwing down their tools and abandoning the big machines the Bayderac had provided. They said, 'What do we need this highway for when we have a thousand ways of our own?' And they set off southward on those old paths and trails.

"You see, all this happened—fortunately, I think—near the end of a northern season. In the north, where we all live apart, and so much of life is spent in courting and making love and bringing up the children, we were—how shall I put it—more shortsighted, more impressionable, more vulnerable. We had just begun the drawing together, then. When we came to the south, when we were all in the Cities under the Sun, we could gather, take counsel together, argue and listen to arguments, and consider what was best for us as a people.

"After we had done that, and had talked further with the Bayderac and let them talk to us, we called for a Great Consensus, such as is spoken of in the legends and the ancient records of the Year Towers where history is kept. Every Ansar came to the Year Tower of their city and voted on this choice: Shall we follow the Bayder Way or the Manad? If we followed their Way, they were to stay among us; if we chose our own, they were to go. We chose our Way." His beak clattered very softly as he laughed. "I was a half-yearling, that season. I cast my vote."

I did not have to ask how he had voted, but I asked if the Bayderac had been willing to go.

"Some of them argued, some of them threatened," he said. "They talked about their wars and their weapons. I am sure they could have destroyed us utterly. But they did not. Maybe they despised us so much they didn't want to bother. Or their wars called them away. By then we had been visited by people from the Interplanary Agency, and most likely it was their doing that the Bayderac left us in peace. Enough of us had been alarmed that we agreed then, in another voting, that we wanted no more visitors. So now the Agency sees to it that they come only to this island. I am not sure we made the right choice, there. Sometimes I think we did, sometimes I wonder. Why are we afraid of other peoples, other Ways? They can't all be like the Bayderac."

"I think you made the right choice," I said. "But I say it against my will. I'd like so much to meet an Ansar woman, to meet your children, to see the Cities under the Sun! I'd like so much to see your dancing!"

"Oh, well, that you can see," he said, and stood up. Maybe we had had a little more ü than usual, that night.

He stood very tall there in the glimmering darkness on the veranda over the beach. He straightened his shoulders, and his head went back. The crest on his head slowly rose into a stiff plume, silver in the starlight. He lifted his arms above his head. It was the pose of the antique Spanish dancer, fiercely elegant, tense, and masculine. He did not leap, he was after all a man of eighty, but he gave somehow the impression of a leap, then a deep graceful bow. His beak clicked out a quick double rhythm, he stamped twice, and his feet seemed to flicker in a complex set of steps while his upper body remained taut and straight. Then his arms came out in a great embracing gesture, towards me, as I sat almost terrified by the beauty and intensity of his dance.

And then he stopped, and laughed. He was out of breath. He sat down and passed his hand over his forehead and his crest, panting a little. "After all," he said, "it isn't courting season."

Social Dreaming of the Frin

NOTE: *Much of the information for this piece comes from* An Oneirological Survey on the Frinthian Plane, *published by Mills College Press, and from conversations with Frinthian scholars and friends.*

O n the Frinthian plane, dreams are not private property. A troubled Frin has no need to lie on a couch recounting dreams to a psychoanalyst, for the doctor already knows what the patient dreamed last night, because the doctor dreamed it too; and the patient also dreamed what the doctor dreamed; and so did everyone else in the neighborhood.

To escape from the dreams of others or to have a private, a

secret dream, the Frin must go out alone into the wilderness. And even in the wilderness, their sleep may be invaded by the strange dream visions of lions, antelope, bears, or mice.

While awake, and during much of their sleep, the Frin are as dream-deaf as we are. Only sleepers who are in or approaching REM sleep can participate in the dreams of others also in REM sleep.

REM is an acronym for "rapid eye movement," a visible accompaniment of this stage of sleep; its signal in the brain is a characteristic type of electroencephalic wave. Most of our rememberable dreams occur during REM sleep.

Frinthian REM sleep and that of people on our plane yield very similar EEG traces, though there are some significant differences, in which may lie the key to the Frinthian ability to share dreams.

To share, the dreamers must be fairly close to one another. The carrying power of the average Frinthian dream is about that of the average human voice. A dream can be received easily within a hundred-meter radius, and bits and fragments of it may carry a good deal farther. A strong dream in a solitary place may well carry for two kilometers or even farther.

In a lonely farmhouse a Frin's dreams mingle only with those of the rest of the family, along with echoes, whiffs, and glimpses of what the cattle in the barn and the dog dozing on the doorstop hear, smell, and see in their sleep.

In a village or town, with people asleep in all the houses around, the Frin spend at least part of every night in a shifting phantasmagoria of their own and other people's dreams which I find hard to imagine.

I asked an acquaintance in a small town to tell me any dreams she could recall from the past night. At first she demurred, saying that they'd all been nonsense, and only "strong" dreams ought to be thought about and talked over. She was evidently reluctant to tell me, an outsider, things that had been going on in her neighbors' heads. I managed at last to convince her that my interest was genuine and not voyeuristic. She thought a while and said, "Well, there was a woman—it was me in the dream, or sort of me, but I think it was the mayor's wife's dream, actually, they live at the corner—this woman, anyhow, and she was trying to find a baby that she'd had last year. She had put the baby into a dresser drawer and forgotten all about it, and now I was, she was, feeling worried about it— Had it had anything to eat? Since last year? Oh my word, how stupid we are in dreams! And then, oh, yes, then there was an awful argument between a naked man and a dwarf, they were in an empty cistern. That may have been my own dream, at least to start with. Because I know that cistern. It was on my grandfather's farm where I used to stay when I was a child. But they both turned into lizards, I think. And then—oh yes!" She laughed. "I was being squashed by a pair of giant breasts, huge ones, with pointy nipples. I think that was the teenage boy next door, because I was terrified but kind of ecstatic, too. And what else was there? Oh, a mouse, it looked so delicious, and it didn't know I was there, and I was just about to pounce, but then there was a horrible thing, a nightmare—a face without any eyes—and huge, hairy hands groping at me—and then I heard the three-year-old next door screaming, because I woke up too. That poor child has so many nightmares, she drives us all crazy. Oh, I don't really like thinking about that one. I'm glad we forget most dreams. Wouldn't it be awful if we had to remember them all!"

Dreaming is a cyclical, not a continuous, activity, and so in small communities there are hours when one's sleep theater, if one may call it so, is dark. REM sleep among settled, local groups of Frin tends to synchronise. As the cycles peak, about five times a night, several or many dreams may be going on simultaneously in everybody's head, intermingling and influencing one another with their mad, inarguable logic, so that (as my friend in the village described it) the baby turns up in the cistern and the mouse hides between the breasts, while the eyeless monster disappears in the dust kicked up by a pig trotting past through a new dream, perhaps a dog's, since the pig is rather dimly seen but is smelled with great particularity. But after such episodes comes a period when everyone can sleep in peace, without anything exciting happening at all.

In Frinthian cities, where one may be within dream range of hundreds of people every night, the layering and overlap of insubstantial imagery is, I'm told, so continual and so confusing that the dreams cancel out, like brushfuls of colors slapped one over the other without design; even one's own dream blurs at once into the meaningless commotion, as if projected on a screen where a hundred films are already being shown, their soundtracks all running together. Only occasionally does a gesture, a voice, ring clear for a moment, or a particularly vivid wet dream or ghastly nightmare cause all the sleepers in a neighborhood to sigh, ejaculate, shudder, or wake up with a gasp.

Frin whose dreams are mostly troubling or disagreeable say they like living in the city for the very reason that their dreams are all but lost in the "stew," as they call it. But others are upset by the constant oneiric noise and dislike spending even a few nights in a metropolis. "I hate to dream strangers' dreams!" my village informant told me. "Ugh! When I come back from staying in the city, I wish I could wash out the inside of my head!"

Even on our plane, young children often have trouble understanding that the experiences they had just before they woke up aren't "real." It must be far more bewildering for Frinthian children, into whose innocent sleep enter the sensations and preoccupations of adults—accidents relived, griefs renewed, rapes reenacted, wrathful conversations held with people fifty years in the grave.

But adult Frin are ready to answer children's questions about the shared dreams and to discuss them, defining them always as dream, though not as unreal. There is no word corresponding to "unreal" in Frinthian; the nearest is "bodiless." So the children learn to live with adults' incomprehensible memories, unmentionable acts, and inexplicable emotions, much as do children who grow up on our plane amid the terrible incoherence of civil war or in times of plague and famine; or, indeed, children anywhere, at any time. Children learn what is real and what isn't, what to notice and what to ignore, as a survival tactic. It is hard for an outsider to judge, but my impression of Frinthian children is that they mature early, psychologically. By the age of seven or eight they are treated by adults as equals.

As for the animals, no one knows what they make of the human dreams they evidently participate in. The domestic beasts of the Frin seemed to me to be remarkably pleasant, trustful, and intelligent. They are generally well looked after. The fact that the Frin share their dreams with their animals might explain why they use animals to haul and plow and for milk and wool, but not as meat.

The Frin say that animals are more sensitive dream receivers than human beings and can receive dreams even from people from other planes. Frinthian farmers have assured me that their cattle and swine are deeply disturbed by the visits of people from carnivorous planes. When I stayed at a farm in Enya Valley the chicken house was in an uproar half the night. I thought it was a fox, but my hosts said it was me.

People who have mingled their dreams all their lives say they are often uncertain where a dream began, whether it was originally theirs or somebody else's; but within a family or village the author of a particularly erotic or ridiculous dream may be all too easily identified. People who know one another well can recognise the source dreamer from the tone or events of the dream, from its style. Still, it has become their own as they dream it. Each dream may be shaped differently in each mind. And, as with us, the personality of the dreamer, the oneiric I, is often tenuous, strangely disguised, or unpredictably different from the daylight person. Very puzzling dreams or those with powerful emotional affect may be discussed on and off all day by the community, without the origin of the dream ever being mentioned.

But most dreams, as with us, are forgotten at waking. Dreams elude their dreamers on every plane.

It might seem to us that the Frin have very little psychic pri-

vacy; but they are protected by this common amnesia, as well as by doubt as to any particular dream's origin and by the obscurity of dream itself. Their dreams are truly common property. The sight of a red-and-black bird pecking at the ear of a bearded human head lying on a plate on a marble table and the rush of almost gleeful horror that accompanied it—did that come from Aunt Unia's sleep, or Uncle Tu's, or Grandfather's, or the cook's, or the girl next door's? A child might ask, "Auntie, did you dream that head?" The stock answer is, "We all did." Which is, of course, the truth.

Frinthian families and small communities are close-knit and generally harmonious, though quarrels and feuds occur. The research group from Mills College that traveled to the Frinthian plane to record and study oneiric brain-wave synchrony agreed that like the synchronisation of menstrual and other cycles within groups on our plane, the communal dreaming of the Frin may serve to establish and strengthen the social bond. They did not speculate as to its psychological or moral effects.

From time to time a Frin is born with unusual powers of projecting and receiving dreams—never one without the other. The Frin call such a dreamer whose signal is unusually clear and powerful a strong mind. That strong-minded dreamers can receive dreams from non-Frinthian humans is a proven fact. Some of them apparently can share dreams with fish, with insects, even with trees. A legendary strong mind named Du Ir claimed that he "dreamed with the mountains and the rivers," but his boast is generally regarded as poetry.

Strong minds are recognised even before birth, when the mother begins to dream that she lives in a warm, amber-colored palace without directions or gravity, full of shadows and complex rhythms and musical vibrations, and shaken often by slow peaceful earthquakes—a dream the whole community enjoys, though late in the pregnancy it may be accompanied by a sense of pressure, of urgency, that rouses claustrophobia in some.

As the strong-minded child grows, its dreams reach two or three times farther than those of ordinary people, and tend to override or co-opt local dreams going on at the same time. The nightmares and inchoate, passionate deliria of a strong-minded child who is sick, abused, or unhappy can disturb everyone in the neighborhood, even in the next village. Such children, therefore, are treated with care; every effort is made to make their life one of good cheer and disciplined serenity. If the family is incompetent or uncaring, the village or town may intervene, the whole community earnestly seeking to ensure the child peaceful days and nights of pleasant dreams.

"World-strong minds" are legendary figures, whose dreams supposedly came to everyone in the world, and who therefore also dreamed the dreams of everyone in the world. Such men and women are revered as holy people, ideals and models for the strong dreamers of today. The moral pressure on strong-minded people is in fact intense, and so must be the psychic pressure. None of them lives in a city: they would go mad, dreaming a whole city's dreams. Mostly they gather in small communities where they live very quietly, widely dispersed from one another at night, practicing the art of "dreaming well," which mostly means dreaming harmlessly. But some of them become guides, philosophers, visionary leaders.

There are still many tribal societies on the Frinthian plane, and the Mills researchers visited several. They reported that among these peoples, strong minds are regarded as seers or shamans, with the usual perquisites and penalties of such eminence. If during a famine the tribe's strong mind dreams of traveling clear down the river and feasting by the sea, the whole tribe may share the vision of the journey and the feast so vividly, with such conviction, that they decide to pack up and start downriver. If they find food along the way, or shellfish and edible seaweeds on the beach, their strong mind gets rewarded with the choice bits; but if they find nothing or run into trouble with other tribes, the seer, now called "the twisted mind," may be beaten or driven out.

The elders told the researchers that tribal councils usually follow the guidance of dream only if other indications favor it. The strong minds themselves urge caution. A seer among the Eastern Zhud-Byu told the researchers, "This is what I say to my people: Some dreams tell us what we wish to believe. Some dreams tell us what we fear. Some dreams are of what we know though we may not know we know it. The rarest dream is the dream that tells us what we have not known."

Frinthia has been open to other planes for over a century, but the rural scenery and quiet lifestyle have brought no great influx of visitors. Many tourists avoid the plane under the impression that the Frin are a race of "mindsuckers" and "psychovoyeurs."

Most Frin are still farmers, villagers, or town dwellers, but the cities and their material technologies are growing fast. Though technologies and techniques can be imported only with the permission of the All-Frin government, requests for such permission by Frinthian companies and individuals have become increasingly frequent. Many Frin welcome this growth of urbanism and materialism, justifying it as the result of the interpretation of dreams received by their strong minds from visitors from other planes. "People came here with strange dreams," says the historian Tubar of Kaps, himself a strong mind. "Our strongest minds joined in them, and joined us with them. So we all began to see things we had never dreamed of. Vast gatherings of people, cybernets, ice cream, much commerce, many pleasant belongings and useful artifacts. 'Shall these remain only dreams?' we said. 'Shall we not bring these things into wakeful being?' So we have done that."

Other thinkers take a more dubious attitude towards alien hypnogogia. What troubles them most is that the dreaming is not reciprocal. For though a strong mind can share the dreams of an alien visitor and "broadcast" them to other Frin, nobody from another plane has been capable of sharing the dreams of the Frin. We cannot enter their nightly festival of fantasies. We are not on their wavelength.

The investigators from Mills hoped to be able to reveal the mechanism by which communal dreaming is effected, but they failed, as Frinthian scientists have also failed, so far. "Telepathy," much hyped in the literature of the interplanary travel agents, is a label, not an explanation. Researchers have established that the genetic programming of all Frinthian mammals includes the capacity for dream sharing, but its operation, though clearly linked to the brain-wave synchrony of sleepers, remains obscure. Visiting foreigners do not synchronise; they do not participate in that nightly ghost chorus of electric impulses dancing to the same beat. But unwittingly, unwillingly—like a deaf child shouting—they send out their own dreams to the strong minds asleep nearby. And to many of the Frin, this seems not so much a sharing as a pollution or infection.

"The purpose of our dreams," says the philosopher Sorrdja of Farfrit, a strong dreamer of the ancient Deyu Retreat, "is to enlarge our souls by letting us imagine all that can be imagined: to release us from the tyranny and bigotry of the individual self by letting us feel the fears, desires, and delights of every mind in every living body near us." The duty of the strong-minded person, she holds, is to strengthen dreams, to focus them—not with a view to practical results or new inventions but as a means of understanding the world through a myriad of experiences and sentiences (not only human). The dreams of the greatest dreamers may offer to those who share them a glimpse of an order underlying all the chaotic stimuli, responses, acts, words, intentions, and imaginings of daily and nightly existence.

"In the day we are apart," she says. "In the night we are together. We should follow our own dreams, not those of strangers who cannot join us in the dark. With such people we can talk; we can learn from them and teach them. We should do so, for that is the way of the daylight. But the way of the night is different. We go together then, apart from them. The dream we dream is our road through the night. They know our day, but not our night, nor the ways we go there. Only we can find our own way, showing one another, following the lantern of the strong mind, following our dreams in darkness."

The resemblance of Sorrdja's phrase "road through the night" to Freud's "royal road to the unconscious" is interesting but, I believe, superficial. Visitors from my plane have discussed psychological theory with the Frin, but neither Freud's nor Jung's views of dream are of much interest to them. The Frinthian "royal road" is trodden not by one secret soul but by a multitude. Repressed feelings, however distorted, disguised, and symbolic, are the common property of everybody in one's household and neighborhood. The Frinthian unconscious, collective or individual, is not a dark wellspring buried deep under years of evasions and denials, but a kind of great moonlit lake to whose shores everybody comes to swim together naked every night.

And so the interpretation of dreams is not, among the Frin, a means of self-revelation, of private psychic inquiry and re-adjustment. It is not even species-specific, since animals share the dreams, though only the Frin can talk about them.

For them, dream is a communion of all the sentient creatures in the world. It puts the notion of self deeply into question. I can imagine only that for them to fall asleep is to abandon the self utterly, to enter or reenter the limitless community of being, almost as death is for us.

The Royals of Hegn

$\approx$

Hegn is a small, cozy plane, blessed with a marvelous climate and a vegetation so rich that lunch or dinner there consists of reaching up to a tree to pluck a succulent, sun-warmed, ripe, rare steakfruit, or sitting down under a llumbush and letting the buttery morsels drop onto one's lap or straight into one's mouth. And then for dessert there are the sorbice blossoms, tart, sweet, and crunchy.

Four or five centuries ago the Hegnish were evidently an enterprising, stirring lot, who built good roads, fine cities, noble country houses and palaces, all surrounded by literally delicious gardens. Then they entered a settling-down phase, and at present they simply live in their beautiful houses. They have hobbies, pursued with tranquil obsession. Some take up the cultivation and breeding of ever finer varieties of grape. (The Hegnian grape is self-fermenting; a small cluster of them has the taste, scent, and effect of a split of Veuve Clicquot. Left longer on the vine, the grapes reach 80 or 90 proof, and the taste comes to resemble single-malt whiskey.) Some raise pet gorkis, an amiable, short-legged domestic animal; others embroider pretty hangings for the churches; many take their pleasure in sports. They all enjoy social gatherings.

People dress nicely for these parties. They eat a few grapes, dance a little, and talk. Conversation is desultory and, some would say, vapid. It concerns the kind and quality of the grapes, discussed with much technicality; the weather, which is usually settled fair but can always be threatening, or have threatened, to rain; and sports, particularly the characteristically Hegnish game of sutpot, which requires a playing field of several acres and involves two teams, many rules, a large ball, several small holes in the ground, a movable fence, a short, flat bat, two vaulting poles, four umpires, and several days. No non-Hegnish person has ever been able to understand sutpot. Hegnishmen discuss the last match played, with the same grave deliberation and relentless attention to detail with which they played it. Other subjects of conversation are the behavior of pet gorkis and the decoration of the local church. Religion and politics are never discussed. It may be that they do not exist, having been reduced to a succession of purely formal events and observances, while their place is filled by the central element, the focus and foundation of Hegnish society, which is best described as the Degree of Consanguinity.

It is a small plane, and nearly everybody on it is related. As it is a monarchy, or rather a congeries of monarchies, this means that almost everybody is, or descended from, a monarch. Everybody is a member of the Royal Family.

In earlier times this universality of aristocracy caused trouble and dissension. Rival claimants to the crown tried to eliminate each other; there was a long period of violence referred to as the Purification of the Peerage, a war called the Agnate War, and the brief, bloody Cross-Cousins' Revolt. But all these family quarrels were settled when the genealogies of every lineage and individual were established and recorded in the great work of the reign of Eduber XII of Sparg, the *Book of the Blood.*

Now 488 years old, this book is, I may say without exaggeration, the centerpiece of every Hegnish household. Indeed it is the only book anybody ever reads. Most people know the sections dealing with their own family by heart. Publication of the annual *Addition and Supplements to the Book of the Blood* is awaited as the great event of the year. It furnishes the staple of conversation for months, as people discuss the sad extinction of the Levigian House with the death of old Prince Levigvig; the exciting possibility of an heir to the Swads arising from the eminently suitable marriage of Endol IV and the Duchess of Mabuber; the unexpected succession of Viscount Lagn to the crown of East Fob due to the untimely deaths of his great-uncle, his uncle, and his cousin all in the same year; or the relegitimisation (by decree of the Board of Editors-Royal) of the great-grandson of the Bastard of Egmorg.

There are 817 kings in Hegn. Each has title to certain lands, or palaces, or at least parts of palaces; but actual rule or dominion over a region isn't what makes a king a king. What matters is having the crown and wearing it on certain occasions, such as the coronation of another king, and having one's lineage recorded unquestionably in the *Book of the Blood,* and edging the sod at the first game of the local sutpot season, and being present at the annual Blessing of the Fish, and knowing that one's wife is the queen and one's eldest son is the crown prince and one's brother is the prince royal and one's sister is the princess royal and all one's relations and all their children are of the blood royal.

To maintain an aristocracy it is necessary that persons of exalted rank form intimate association only with others of their kind. Fortunately there are plenty of those. Just as the bloodline of a Thoroughbred horse on my plane can be tracked straight back to the Godolphin Arabian, every royal family of Hegn can trace its descendance from Rugland of Hegn-Glander, who ruled eight centuries ago. The horses don't care, but their owners do, and so do the kings and the royal families. In this sense, Hegn may be seen as a vast stud farm.

There is an unspoken consensus that certain royal houses are slightly, as it were, more royal than others, because they descend directly from Rugland's eldest son rather than one of his eight younger sons; but all the other royal houses have married into the central line often enough to establish an unshakable connection. Each house also has some unique, incomparable claim to distinction, such as descent from Alfign the Ax, the semi-legendary conqueror of North Hegn, or a collateral saint, or a family tree never sullied by marriage with a mere duke or duchess but exhibiting (on the ever-open page of the *Book of the Blood* in the palace library) a continuous and unadulterated flowering of true blue princes and princesses.

And so, when the novelty of the annual *Addition and Supplements* at last wears thin, the royal guests at the royal parties can always fall back on discussing degrees of consanguinity, settling such questions as whether the son born of Agnin IV's second marriage, to Tivand of Shut, was or was not the same prince who was slain at the age of thirteen defending his father's palace against the Anti-Agnates and therefore could, or could not, have been the father of the Duke of Vigrign, later King of Shut.

Such questions are not of interest to everyone, and the placid fanaticism with which the Hegnish pursue them bores or offends many visitors to their plane. The fact that the Hegnish have absolutely no interest in any people except themselves can also cause offense, or even rage. Foreigners exist. That is all the Hegnish know about them, and all they care to know. They are too polite to say that it is a pity that foreigners exist, but if they had to think about it, they would think so.

They do not, however, have to think about foreigners. That is taken care of for them. The Interplanary Hotel on Hegn is in Hemgogn, a beautiful little kingdom on the west coast. The Interplanary Agency runs the hotel and hires local guides. The guides, mostly dukes and earls, take visitors to see the Alternation of the Watch on the Walls, performed by princes of the blood, wearing magnificent traditional regalia, at noon and six daily. The Agency also offers day tours to a couple of other kingdoms. The bus runs softly along the ancient, indestructible roads among sunlit orchards and wildfood forests. The tourists get out of the bus and look at the ruins, or walk through the parts of the palace open to visitors. The inhabitants of the palace are aloof but unfailingly civil and courteous, as befits royalty. Perhaps the Queen comes down and smiles at the tourists without actually looking at them and instructs the pretty little Crown Princess to invite them to pick and eat whatever they like in the lunch orchard, and then she and the Princess go back into the private part of the palace, and the tourists have lunch and get back into the bus. And that is that.

Being an introvert, I rather like Hegn. One does not have to mingle, since one can't. And the food is good, and the sunlight sweet. I went there more than once, and stayed longer than most people do, and so it happened that I learned about the Hegnish Commoners.

I was walking down the main street of Legners Royal, the capital of Hemgogn, when I saw a crowd in the square in front of the old Church of the Thrice Royal Martyr. I thought it must be one of the many annual festivals or rituals and joined the crowd to watch. These events are always slow, decorous, and profoundly dull. But they're the only events there are; and they have their own tedious charm. Soon, however, I saw this was a funeral. And it was altogether different from any Hegnish ceremony I had ever witnessed, above all in the behavior of the people.

They were all royals, of course, like any crowd in Hegn, all of them princes, dukes, earls, princesses, duchesses, countesses, etc. But they were not behaving with the regal reserve, the sovereign aplomb, the majestic apathy I had always seen in them before. They were standing about in the square, for once not engaged in any kind of prescribed ritual duty or traditional occupation or hobby, but just crowding together, as if for comfort.

They were disturbed, distressed, disorganised, and verged upon being noisy. They showed emotion. They were grieving, openly grieving.

The person nearest me in the crowd was the Dowager Duchess of Mogn and Farstis, the Queen's aunt by marriage. I knew who she was because I had seen her, every morning at half past eight, issue forth from the Royal Palace to walk the King's pet gorki in the palace gardens, which border on the hotel. One of the Agency guides had told me who she was. I had watched from the window of the breakfast room of the hotel while the gorki, a fine, heavily testicled specimen, relieved himself under the cheeseblossom bushes, and the Dowager Duchess gazed away into a tranquil vacancy reserved for the eyes of true aristocrats.

But now those pale eyes were filled with tears, and the soft, weathered face of the Duchess worked with the effort to control her feelings.

"Your ladyship," I said, hoping that the translatomat would provide the proper appellation for a duchess in case I had it wrong, "forgive me, I am from another country, whose funeral is this?"

She looked at me unseeing, dimly surprised but too absorbed in sorrow to wonder at my ignorance or my effrontery. "Sissie's," she said, and speaking the name made her break into open sobs for a moment. She turned away, hiding her face in her large lace handkerchief, and I dared ask no more.

The crowd was growing rapidly, constantly. By the time the coffin was borne forth from the church, there must have been over a thousand people, most of the population of Legners, all of them members of the Royal Family, crowded into the square. The King and his two sons and his brother followed the coffin at a respectful distance.

The coffin was carried and closely surrounded by people I had never seen before, a very odd lot—pale, fat men in cheap suits, pimply boys, middle-aged women with brassy hair and stiletto heels, and a highly visible young woman with thick thighs. She wore a miniskirt, a halter top, and a black cotton lace mantilla. She staggered along after the coffin, weeping aloud, half hysterical, supported on one side by a scared-looking man with a pencil mustache and two-tone shoes, on the other by a small, dry, tired, dogged woman in her seventies dressed entirely in rusty black.

At the far edge of the crowd I saw a native guide with whom I had struck up a lightweight friendship, a young viscount, son of the Duke of Ist, and I worked my way towards him. It took quite a while, as everyone was streaming along with the slow procession of the coffin bearers and their entourage towards the King's limousines and horse-drawn coaches that waited near the palace gates. When I finally got to the guide, I said, "Who is it? Who are they?"

"Sissie," he said almost in a wail, caught up in the general grief—"Sissie died last night!" Then, coming back to his duties as guide and interpreter and trying to regain his pleasant aristo-cratic manner, he looked at me, blinked back his tears, and said, "They're our commoners."

"And Sissie—?"

"She's, she was, their daughter. The only daughter." Do

what he could, the tears would well into his eyes. "She was such a dear girl. Such a help to her mother, always. Such a sweet smile. And there's nobody like her, nobody. She was the only one. Oh, she was so full of love. Our poor little Sissie!" And he broke right down and cried aloud.

At this moment the King and his sons and brother passed quite close to us. I saw that both the boys were weeping, and that the King's stony face betrayed a superhuman effort to maintain calm. His slightly retarded brother appeared to be in a daze, holding tight to the King's arm and walking beside him like an automaton.

The crowd poured after the funeral procession. People pushed in closer, trying to touch the fringes of the white silk pall over the coffin. "Sissie! Sissie!" voices cried. "Oh, Mother, we loved her too!" they cried. "Dad, Dad, what are we going to do without her? She's with the angels," the voices cried. "Don't cry, Mother, we love you! We'll always love you! Oh Sissie! Sissie! Our own sweet girl!"

Slowly, hampered, almost prevented by the passionate protestations of the immense royal family gathered about it, the coffin and its attendants reached the coaches and cars. When the coffin was slid into the back of the long white hearse, a quavering, inhuman moan went up from every throat. Noblewomen screamed in thin, high voices and noblemen fainted away. The girl in the miniskirt fell into what looked like an epileptic fit, foaming at the mouth, but she recovered quite quickly, and one of the fat, pale men shoved her into a limousine.

The engines of the cars purred, the coachmen stirred up their handsome white horses, and the cortege set off, slowly still, at a foot pace. The crowd poured after it.

I went back to the hotel. I learned that evening that most of the population of the city of Legners Royal had followed the cortege all the way, six miles, to the graveyard, and stood through the burial service and the inhumation. All through the evening, late at night, people were still straggling back towards the palace and the royal apartments, weary, footsore, tear-stained.

During the next few days I talked with the young viscount, who was able to explain to me the phenomenon I had witnessed. I had understood that all the people in the Kingdom of Hemgogn were of royal blood, directly related to its (and other) kings; what I had not known was that there was one family who were not royal. They were common. Their name was Gat.

That surname, and Mrs. Gat's maiden name, Tugg, went entirely unmentioned in the *Book of the Blood*. No Gat or Tugg had ever married anybody royal or even noble. There was no family legend about a handsome young prince who seduced the fair daughter of the bootmaker. There were no family legends. There was no family history. The Gats didn't know where they came from or how long they had lived in the kingdom. They were bootmakers by trade. Few people in sunny Hegn ever wear boots. As his father had done, and as his son was learning to do, Mr. Gat made dressy leather boots for the Princes of the Watch, and ugly felt boots for the Queen Mother, who liked to walk in the smallmeat meadows in winter with her gorkis. Uncle Agby knew how to tan leather. Aunt Irs knew how to felt wool. Great-Aunt Yoly raised sheep. Cousin Fafvig ate far too many grapes and was drunk most of the time. The eldest daughter, Chickie, was a bit wild, though good at heart. And Sissie, sweet Sissie, the younger daughter, had been the kingdom's darling, the Wild Flower of Hemgogn, the Little Common Girl.

She had always been delicate. The story was that she had fallen in love with young Prince Frodig, though he of course could never have married her. It was said they had been seen talking, once, more than once, near the Palace Bridge at twilight. My viscount clearly wanted to believe this but found it difficult, since Prince Frodig had been out of the country, at school in Halfvig, for three years. At any rate, Sissie had a weak chest. "The commoners often do," the viscount said, "it's hereditary. Runs in the female line." She had gone into a decline, grown wan and pale, never complaining, always smiling but so thin and quiet, just faded away, from day to day, until she lay, in the cold cold clay, Sweet Sissie, the Wild Flower of Hemgogn.

And the whole kingdom mourned her. They mourned her wildly, extravagantly, unconsolably, royally. The King had wept at her open grave. Just before they began to shovel in the earth, the Queen had laid on Sissie's coffin the diamond brooch that had come down to her, mother to daughter, for seventeen generations from Erbinrasa of the North, a jewel that no hand had ever touched that was not of the blood of the Erbinnas. Now it lay in the grave of the Little Common Girl. "It was not as bright as her eyes," the Queen said.

I had to leave Hegn not long after this funeral. Other travels absorbed me for three or four years, and when I went back to the Kingdom of Hemgogn, the orgy of grief was long over. I looked up my viscount. He had given up playing at being a guide upon coming into his inheritance: the title of Duke of Ist and an apartment in the New Wing of the Royal Palace, with usufruct of one of the Royal Vineyards, which furnished grapes for his parties.

He was a nice young man, with a faint strain of originality in him that had led him to his avocation as a guide; he was actually well disposed towards foreigners. He also had a kind of helpless politeness, which I took advantage of. He was quite incapable of refusing a direct request, and so, because I asked him to, he invited me to several parties during the month I stayed in Hemgogn.

It was then that I discovered the other subject of conversation in Hegn—the topic that could eclipse sports, gorkis, the weather, and even consanguinity.

The Tuggs and the Gats, of whom there were nineteen or twenty at that time, were of inexhaustible, absorbing interest to the royalty of Hemgogn. Children made scrapbooks about them. The Viscount's mother had a cherished mug and plate bearing portraits of "Mother" and "Dad" Gat on their wedding day, surrounded by gilt scrolls. Rather amateurish mimeographed reports of the Common Family's doings and snapshots of them made by the royals of Hemgogn were enormously popular not only throughout the kingdom but also in the neighboring kingdoms of Drohe and Vigmards, neither of which had a family of commoners. The larger neighboring reign to the south, Odboy, had three common families and an actual, living wastrel, called the Old Tramp of Odboy. Yet even there, gossip about the Gats, how short Chickie's skirts were, how long Mother Tugg seethed her underwear, whether Uncle Agby had a tumor or only a boil, whether Auntie and Uncle Bod were going to the seashore for a week in summer or an excursion to the Vigmards Hills in autumn—all this was discussed almost as eagerly in Odboy as in the commonerless kingdoms or Hemgogn itself. And a portrait of Sissie wearing a crown of wildflowers, made from a snapshot that was said to have been taken by Prince Frodig, though Chickie insisted that she had taken it, adorned the walls of a thousand rooms in a dozen palaces.

I met a few royals who did not share the general adoration. Old Prince Foford took rather a liking to me, foreigner as I was. The King's first cousin and my friend the Duke's uncle, he prided himself on his unconventionality, his radical thinking. "Rebel of the Family, they call me," he said in his growly voice, his eyes twinkling among wrinkles. He raised flennis, not gorkis, and had no patience at all with the Commoners, not even Sissie. "Weak," he growled, "no stamina. No breeding. Flaunted herself about under the walls, hoping the Prince'd see her. Caught cold, died of it. Whole lot of 'em sickly. Sickly, ignorant beggars. Filthy houses. Put on a show, that's all they know how to do. Dirt, screeching, flinging pots, black eyes, foul language—all show. All humbug. Couple of dukes in that woodpile, back a generation or two. Know it for a fact."

And indeed, as I took notice of the gossip, the bulletins, the photographs, and of the Commoners themselves as they went about the streets of Legners Royal, they did seem rather insistently, even blatantly lower-class: *professional* is perhaps the term I want. No doubt Chickie had not deliberately planned to be impregnated by her uncle, but when she was, she certainly made the most of it. She would tell any prince or princess with a notebook the woeful tale of how Uncle Tugg had squashed half-rotted grapes into her mouth till she was vomiting drunk and then tore off her clothes and screwed her. The story grew with the telling, getting more and more steamy and explicit. It was the thirteen-year-old Prince Hodo who wrote down Chickie's vivid words concerning the brutal weight of Uncle Tugg's hairy body and how even as she fought him her own body betrayed her, her nipples hardening and her thighs parting as he forced his, and here the prince put four asterisks, into her four asterisks. To one of the younger duchesses Chickie confessed that she had tried to get rid of the baby but hot baths were a bunch of crap and Grandma's herbs were a load of shit and you could kill yourself with knitting needles. Meanwhile Uncle Tugg went around boasting that the family had always called him Fuckemall, until his brother-in-law, Chickie's putative father (there was a good deal of doubt concerning Chickie's parentage, and Uncle Tugg himself may have been her father), lay in wait for him, attacked him from behind with a piece of lead pipe, and beat him senseless. The entire kingdom shuddered voluptuously when Uncle Tugg was discovered lying in a pool of blood and urine at the door of the family outhouse.

For the Gats and Tuggs had no plumbing, no running water, no electricity. The previous queen, in a misplaced fit of compassion or noblesse oblige, had had wiring installed in the main house of the ancient, filthy warren of hovels and sheds called the Commons, where snot-nosed urchins played in gutted automobiles and huge dogs lunged on short chains in endless frenzies of barking, trying to attack Great-Aunt Yoly's mangy sheep that wandered about among the stinking vats of Uncle Agby's tannery. The boys broke all the lightbulbs with their slingshots the first day. Gamma Gat would never use the electric oven, preferring to roast her breadfruit in the cavernous woodstove. Mice and rats ate the insulation and shorted out the circuits. The principal result of the electrification of the Commons was a lingering stink of fried rat.

As a rule the Commoners avoided foreigners with blank inattention, just as the royals did. Now and then their patriotic bigotry boiled up and they threw garbage at tourists. Informed of this, the Palace always issued a brief statement of shock and dismay that Hegnishmen should so forget the hospitable traditions of the kingdom. But at the royal parties there was often a little satisfied sniggering and murmurs of "Gave the beggars a bit of their own, eh?" For after all, tourists were commoners; but they weren't *our* commoners.

Our commoners had picked up one foreign habit. They all smoked American cigarettes from the age of six or seven, and had yellow fingers, bad breath, and horrible phlegmy coughs. Cousin Cadge, one of the fat, pale men I had seen at the funeral, ran a profitable cigarette-smuggling business through his dwarfish son Stumpy, who was employed to clean toilets at the Interplanary Hotel. Young royals often bought cigarettes from Cadge and smoked them in secret, relishing the nausea, the nastiness, the sense of being for a few minutes real vulgarians, genuine scum.

I left before Chickie's baby was born, but royal attention was already centered on the coming event, and was only heightened by Chickie's frequent public announcements that she was sure the little bastard would be a drooling idiot born without any arms or legs or four asterisks, what else could you expect. And the royal families of four kingdoms did not want to expect anything else. Fascinated, appalled, they looked forward to a genetic disaster, a tiny, monstrous plebeian to cluck and sigh and shudder over. I am sure Chickie did her duty and provided them one.

Woeful Tales from Mahigul

When I'm in Mahigul, a peaceful place nowadays though it has a bloody history, I spend most of my time at the Imperial Library. Many would consider this a dull thing to do when on another plane, or indeed anywhere; but I, like Borges, think of heaven as something very like a library.

Most of the Library of Mahigul is outdoors. The archives, bookstacks, electronic storage units, and computers for the legemats are all housed underground in vaults where temperature and humidity can be controlled, but above this vast complex rise airy arcades forming walks and shelters around many plots and squares and parklands—the Reading Gardens of the Library. Some are paved courtyards, orderly and secluded, like a cloister. Others are broad parks with dells and little hills, groves of trees, open lawns, and grassy glades sheltered by hedges of flowering shrubs. All are very quiet. They're never crowded; one can talk with a friend, or have a group discussion; there's usually a poet shouting away somewhere on the grounds, but there's perfect solitude for those who want it. The courtyards and patios always have a fountain, sometimes a silent, welling pool, sometimes a series of bowls, the water cascading from basin to basin. Through the larger parks wind the many branches of a clear stream, with little falls here and there. You always hear the sound of water. Unobtrusive, comfortable seats are provided, light chairs that can be moved, some of them legless, just a frame with a canvas seat and back, so you can sit right on the short green turf but have your back supported while you read; and there are chairs and tables and chaise longues in the shade of the trees and under the arcades. All these seats are provided with outlets into which you can connect your legemat.

The climate of Mahigul is lovely, dry, and hot all summer and fall. In spring, during the mild, steady rains, big awnings are stretched from one library arcade to the next, so that you can still sit outdoors, hearing the soft drumming on the canvas overhead, looking up from your reading to see the trees and the pale sky beyond the awning. Or you can settle down under the stone arches that surround a quiet, grey courtyard and see rain patter in the lily-dotted central pool. In winter it's often foggy, not a cold fog but a mist through which and in which the sunlight is always warmly palpable, like the color in a milk opal. The fog softens the sloping lawns and the high, dark trees, bringing them close, into a quiet, mysterious intimacy.

So when I'm in Mahigul I go there, and greet the patient,

knowledgeable librarians, and browse around in the findery until I find an interesting bit of fiction or history. History, usually, because the history of Mahigul outdoes the fiction of many other places. It is a sad and violent history, but in so sweet and lenient a place as the Reading Gardens it seems both possible and wise to open one's heart to folly, pain, and sorrow. These are a few of the stories I've read sitting in the mild autumn sunlight on the grassy edge of a stream, or in the deep shade of a silent, secret little patio on a hot summer afternoon, in the Library of Mahigul.

DAWODOW THE INNUMERABLE

When Dawodow, Fiftieth Emperor of the Fourth Dynasty of Mahigul, came to the throne, many statues of his grandfather Andow and his father Dowwode stood in the capital city and the lesser cities of the land. Dawodow ordered them all recarved into his own image, so that they all became portraits of him. He also had countless new likenesses of himself carved. Thousands of workmen were employed at immense stoneyards and workshops making idealised portrait figures of the Emperor Dawodow. What with the old statues with new faces and the new statues, there were so many that there weren't pedestals and plinths enough to set them on or niches enough to set them in, so they were placed on sidewalks, at street crossings, on the steps of temples and public buildings, and in squares and plazas. As the Emperor kept paying the sculptors to carve the statues and the stoneyards kept turning them out, soon there were too many to place singly; groups and crowds of Dawodows now stood motionless among the people going about their business in every town and city of the kingdom. Even small villages had ten or a dozen Dawodows, standing in the high street or the side lanes, among the pigs and chickens.

At night the Emperor would often put on plain, dark clothing and leave the palace by a secret door. Officers of the palace guard followed him at a distance to protect him during these nocturnal excursions through his capital city (called, at that time, Dawodowa). They and other palace officials witnessed his behavior many times. The Emperor would go about in the streets and plazas of the capital, and stop at every image or group of images of himself. He would jeer softly at the statues, insulting them in a whisper, calling them coward, fool, cuckold, impotent, idiot. He would spit on a statue as he passed it. If he saw no one else in the plaza, he would stop and piss on the statue, or piss on earth to make mud and then, taking this mud in his hand, rub it on the face of the image of himself and over the inscription extolling the glories of his reign.

If a citizen reported next day that he had seen an image of the Emperor defiled in this way, the guards would arrest a countryman or a foreigner, anyone who came to hand—if nobody else was convenient, they arrested the citizen who had reported the crime—accuse him of sacrilege, and torture him until he died or confessed. If he confessed, the Emperor in his capacity as God's Judge would condemn him to die in the next mass Execution of Justice. These executions took place every forty days. The Emperor, his priests, and his court watched them. Since the victims were strangled one by one by garotte, the ceremony often lasted several hours.

The Emperor Dawodow reigned for thirty-seven years. He was garotted in his privy by his great-nephew Danda.

During the civil wars that followed, most of the thousands of statues of Dawodow were destroyed. A group of them in front of the temple in a small city in the mountains stood for many centuries, worshiped by the local people as images of the Nine Blessed Guides to the Inworld. Constant rubbing of sweet oil on the images obliterated the faces entirely, reducing the heads to featureless lumps, but enough of the inscription remained that a scholar of the Seventh Dynasty could identify them as the last remnants of the Innumerable Dawodow.

THE CLEANSING OF OBTRY

Obtry is currently a remote western province of the Empire of Mahigul. It was absorbed when Emperor Tro II annexed the nation of Ven, which had previously annexed Obtry.

The Cleansing of Obtry began about five hundred years ago, when Obtry, a democracy, elected a president whose campaign promise was to drive the Astasa out of the country.

At that time, the rich plains of Obtry had been occupied for over a millennium by two peoples: the Sosa, who had come from the northwest, and the Astasa, who had come from the southwest. The Sosa arrived as refugees, driven from their homeland by invaders, at about the same time the seminomadic Astasa began to settle down in the grazing lands of Obtry.

Displaced by these immigrants, the aboriginal inhabitants of Obtry, the Tyob, retreated to the mountains, where they lived as poor herdsfolk. The Tyob kept to their old primitive ways and language and were not allowed to vote.

The Sosa and the Astasa each brought a religion to the plains of Obtry. The Sosa prostrated themselves in worship of a father-god called Af. The highly formal rituals of the Affa religion were held in temples and led by priests. The Astasa religion was nontheistic and unprofessional, involving trances, whirling dances, visions, and small fetishes.

When they first came to Obtry the Astasa were fierce warriors, driving the Tyob up into the mountains and taking the best farmlands from the Sosa settlers; but there was plenty of good land, and the two invading peoples gradually settled down side by side. Cities were built along the rivers, some of them populated by Sosa, some by Astasa. The Sosa and Astasa traded, and their trade increased. Sosa traders soon began to live in enclaves or ghettos in Astasa cities, and Astasa traders began to live in enclaves or ghettos in Sosa cities.

For over nine hundred years there was no central government over the region. It was a congeries of city-states and farm territories, which competed in trade with one another and from time to time quarreled or battled over land or belief, but generally maintained a watchful, thriving peace.

The Astasa opinion of the Sosa was that they were slow, dense, deceitful, and indefatigable. The Sosa opinion of the Astasa was that they were quick, clever, candid, and unpredictable.

The Sosa learned how to play the wild, whining, yearning music of the Astasa. The Astasa learned contour plowing and crop rotation from the Sosa. They seldom, however, learned each other's language—only enough to trade and bargain with, some insults, and some words of love.

Sons of the Sosa and daughters of the Astasa fell madly in love and ran off together, breaking their mothers' hearts. Astasa boys eloped with Sosa girls, the curses of their families filling the skies and darkening the streets behind them. These fugitives went to other cities, where they lived in Affastasa enclaves and Sosasta or Astasosa ghettos, and brought up their children to prostrate themselves to Af, or to whirl in the fetish dance. The Affastasa did both, on different holy days. The Sosasta performed whirling dances to a wild whining music before the altar of Af, and the Astasosa prostrated themselves to little fetishes.

The Sosa, the unadulterated Sosa who worshiped Af in the ancestral fashion and who mostly lived on farms not in the cities, were instructed by their priests that their God wished them to bear sons in His honor; so they had large families. Many priests had four or five wives and twenty or thirty children. Devout Sosa women prayed to Father Af for a twelfth, a fifteenth baby. In contrast, an Astasa woman bore a child only when she had been told, in trance, by her own body fetish, that it was a good time to conceive; and so she seldom had more than two or three children. Thus the Sosa came to outnumber the Astasa.

About five hundred years ago, the unorganised cities, towns, and farming communities of Obtry, under pressure from the aggressive Vens to the north and under the influence of the Ydaspian Enlightenment emanating from the Mahigul Empire in the east, drew together and formed first an alliance, then a nation-state. Nations were in fashion at the time. The Nation of Obtry was established as a democracy, with a president, a cabinet, and a parliament elected by universal adult suffrage. The parliament proportionately represented the regions (rural and urban) and the ethnoreligious populations (Sosa, Astasa, Affastasa, Sosasta, and Astasosa).

The fourth President of Obtry was a Sosa named Diud, elected by a fairly large majority.

Although his campaign had become increasingly outspoken against "godless" and "foreign" elements of Obtrian society, many Astasa voted for him. They wanted a strong leader, they said. They wanted a man who would stand up against the Vens and restore law and order to the cities, which were suffering from overpopulation and uncontrolled mercantilism.

Within half a year Diud, having put personal favorites in the key positions in the cabinet and parliament and consolidated his control of the armed forces, began his campaign in earnest. He instituted a universal census which required all citizens to state their religious allegiance (Sosa, Sosasta, Astasosa, or Heathen) and their bloodline (Sosa or non-Sosa).

Diud then moved the Civic Guard of Dobaba, a predominately Sosa city in an almost purely Sosa agricultural area, to the city of Asu, a major river port, where the population had lived peacefully in Sosa, Astasa, Sosasta, and Astasosa neighborhoods for centuries. There the guards began to force all Astasa, or Heathen non-Sosa, newly reidentified as godless persons, to leave their homes, taking with them only what they could seize in the terror of sudden displacement.

The godless persons were shipped by train to the northwestern border. There they were held in various fenced camps or pens for weeks or months, before being taken to the Venian border. They were dumped from trucks or train cars and ordered to cross the border. At their backs were soldiers with guns. They obeyed. But there were also soldiers facing them: Ven border guards. The first time this happened, the Ven soldiers, thinking they were facing an Obtrian invasion, shot hundreds of people before they realised that most of the invaders were children or babies or old or pregnant, that none of them were armed, that all of them were cowering, crawling, trying to run away, crying for mercy. Some of the Ven soldiers continued shooting anyway, on the principle that Obtrians were the enemy.

President Diud continued his campaign of rounding up all the godless persons, city by city. Most were taken to remote regions and kept herded in fenced areas called instructional centers, where they were supposed to be instructed in the worship of Af. Little shelter and less food was provided in the instructional centers. Most of the inmates died within a year. Many Astasa fled before the roundups, heading for the border and risking the random mercy of the Vens. By the end of his first term of office, President Diud had cleansed his nation of half a million Astasa.

He ran for reelection on the strength of his record. No Astasa candidate dared run. Diud was narrowly defeated by the new favorite of the rural, religious Sosa voters, Riusuk. Riusuk's campaign slogan was "Obtry for God," and his particular target was the Sosasta communities in the southern cities and towns, whose dancing worship his followers held to be particularly evil and sacrilegious.

A good many soldiers in the southern province, however, were Sosasta, and in Riusuk's first year of office they mutinied. They were joined by guerrilla and partisan Astasa groups hiding out in the forests and inner cities. Unrest and violence spread and factions multiplied. President Riusuk was kidnapped from his lakeside summer house. After a week his mutilated body was found beside a highway. Astasa fetishes had been stuffed into his mouth, ears, and nostrils.

During the turmoil that ensued, an Astasosa general, Hodus, naming himself acting president, took control of a large splinter group of the army and instituted a Final Cleansing of Godless Atheist Heathens, the term which now defined Astasa, Sosasta, and Affastasa. His soldiers killed anybody who was or was thought to be or was said to be non-Sosa, shooting them wherever they were found and leaving the bodies to rot.

Affastasa from the northwestern province took arms under an able leader, Shamato, who had been a schoolteacher; her partisans, fiercely loyal, held four northern cities and the mountain regions against Hodus's forces for seven years. Shamato was killed on a raid into Astasosa territory.

Hodus closed the universities as soon as he took power. He installed Affan priests as teachers in the schools, but later in the civil war all schools shut down, as they were favorite targets for sharpshooters and bombers. There were no safe trade routes, the borders were closed, commerce ceased, famine followed, and epidemics followed famine. Sosa and non-Sosa continued killing one another.

The Vens invaded the northern province in the sixth year of the civil war. They met almost no resistance, as all able-bodied men and women were dead or fighting their neighbors. The Ven army swept through Obtry cleaning out pockets of resistance. The region was annexed to the Nation of Ven, and remained a tributary province for the next several centuries.

The Vens, contemptuous of all Obtrian religions, enforced public worship of their deity, the Great Mother of the Teats. The Sosa, Astasosa, and Sosasta learned to prostrate themselves before huge mammary effigies, and the few remaining Astasa and Affastasa learned to dance in a circle about small tit fetishes.

Only the Tyob, far up in the mountains, remained much as they had always been, poor herdsfolk, with no religion worth fighting over. The anonymous author of the great mystical poem *The Ascent,* a work which has made the province of Obtry famous on more than one plane, was a Tyob.

THE BLACK DOG

Two tribes of the great Yeye Forest were traditional enemies. As a boy of the Hoa or the Farim grew up, he could scarcely wait for the honor of being chosen to go on a raid—the seal and recognition of his manhood.

Most raids were met by an opposing war party from the other tribe, and the battles were fought on various traditional battlegrounds, clearings in the forested hills and river valleys where the Hoa and Farim lived. After hard fighting, when six or seven men had been wounded or killed, the war chiefs on both sides would simultaneously declare a victory. The warriors of each tribe would run home, carrying their dead and wounded, to hold a victory dance. The dead warriors were propped up to watch the dance before they were buried.

Occasionally, by some mistake in communications, no war party came forth to meet the raiders, who were then obliged to run on into the enemy's village and kill men and carry off women and children for slaves. This was unpleasant work and often resulted in the death of women, children, and old people of the village as well as the loss of many of the raiding party. It was considered much more satisfactory all around if the raidees knew that the raiders were coming, so that the fighting and killing could be done properly on a battlefield and did not get out of hand.

The Hoa and Farim had no domestic animals except small terrier-like dogs to keep the huts and granaries free of mice. Their weapons were short bronze swords and long wooden lances, and they carried hide shields. Like Odysseus, they used bow and arrow for sport and for hunting but not in battle. They planted grain and root vegetables in clearings, and moved the village to new planting grounds every five or six years. Women and girls did all the farming, gathering, food preparation, house moving, and other work, which was not called work but "what women do." The women also did the fishing. Boys snared wood rats and coneys, men hunted the small roan deer of the forest, and old men decided when it was time to plant, when it was time to move the village, and when it was time to send a raid against the enemy.

So many young men were killed in raids that there were not many old men to argue about these matters, and if they did get into an argument about planting or moving, they could always agree to order another raid.

Since the beginning of time things had gone along in this fashion, with raids once or twice a year, both sides celebrating victory. Word of a raid was usually leaked well in advance, and the raiding party sang war songs very loudly as they came; so the battles were fought on the battlefields, the villages were unharmed, and the villagers had only to mourn their fallen heroes and declare their undying hatred of the vile Hoa, or the vile Farim. It was all satisfactory, until the Black Dog appeared.

The Farim got word that Hoa was sending out a large war party. All the Farim warriors stripped naked, seized their swords, lances, and shields, and singing war songs loudly, rushed down the forest trail to the battlefield known as By Bird Creek. There they met the men of the Hoa just running into the clearing, naked, armed with lance, sword, and shield, singing war songs loudly.

But in front of the Hoa came a strange thing: a huge black dog. Its back was as high as a man's waist, and its head was massive. It ran in leaps and bounds, its eyes gleamed red, foam slathered from its gaping, long-toothed jaws, and it growled hideously. It attacked the war chief of the Farim, jumping straight at his chest. It knocked him down, and even as he tried vainly to stab it with his sword, the dog tore open his throat.

This utterly unexpected, untraditional, horrible event bewildered and terrified the Farim, paralysed them. Their war song died away. They barely resisted the assault of the Hoa. Four more Farim men and boys were killed—one of them by the Black Dog—before they fled in panic, scattering through the forest, not stopping to pick up their dead.

Such a thing had never happened before.

The old men of the Farim therefore had to discuss the matter very deeply before they ordered a retaliatory raid.

Since raids were always victorious, usually months went by, sometimes even a year, before another battle was needed to keep the young men in heroic fettle; but this was different. The Farim had been defeated. Their warriors had had to creep back to the battleground at night, in fear and trembling, to pick up their dead; and they found the bodies defiled by the dog—one man's ear had been chewed off, and the war chief's left arm had been eaten, its bones lying about, tooth-marked.

The need of the warriors of the Farim to win a victory was urgent. For three days and nights the old men sang war songs. Then the young men stripped, took up their swords, lances, shields, and ran, grim-faced and singing loudly, down the forest path towards the village of the Hoa.

But even before they got to the first battlefield on that path, bounding towards them on the narrow trail under the trees came the terrible Black Dog. Following it came the warriors of the Hoa, singing loudly.

The warriors of the Farim turned around and ran away without fighting, scattering through the forest.

One by one they straggled into their village, late in the evening. The women did not greet them but set out food for them silently. Their children turned away from them and hid from them in the huts. The old men also stayed in the huts, crying.

The warriors lay down, each alone on his sleeping mat, and they too cried.

The women talked in the starlight by the drying racks. "We will all be made slaves," they said. "Slaves of the vile Hoa. Our children will be slaves."

No raid, however, came from the Hoa, the next day, or the next. The waiting was very difficult. Old men and young men talked together. They decided that they must raid the Hoa and kill the Black Dog even if they died in the attempt.

They sang the war songs all night long. In the morning, very grim-faced and not singing, they set out, all the warriors of Farim, on the straightest trail to Hoa. They did not run. They walked, steadily.

They looked and looked ahead, down the trail, for the Black Dog to appear, with its red eyes and slathering jaws and gleaming teeth. In dread they looked for it.

And it appeared. But it was not leaping and bounding at them, snarling and growling. It ran out from the trees into the path and stopped a moment looking back at them, silent, with what seemed a grin on its terrible mouth. Then it set off trotting ahead of them.

"It is running from us," cried Ahu.

"It is leading us," said Yu, the war chief.

"Leading us to death," said young Gim.

"To victory!" Yu cried, and began to run, holding his spear aloft.

They were at the Hoa village before the Hoa men realised it was a raid and ran out to meet them, clothed, unready, unarmed. The Black Dog leapt at the first Hoa man, knocked him onto his back, and began tearing at his face and throat. Children and women of the village screamed, some ran away, some seized sticks and tried to attack the attackers, all was confusion, but all of them fled when the Black Dog left his victim and charged at the villagers. The warriors of the Farim followed the Black Dog into the village. There they killed several men and seized two women all in a moment. Then Yu shouted, "Victory!" and all his warriors shouted, "Victory!" and they turned and set off back to Farim, carrying their captives, but not their dead, for they had not lost a man.

The last warrior in line looked back down the trail. The Black Dog was following them. Its mouth dropped white saliva.

At Farim they held a victory dance; but it was not a satisfactory victory dance. There were no dead warriors propped up, bloody sword in cold hand, to watch and approve the dancers. The two slaves they had taken sat with their heads bowed and their hands over their eyes, crying. Only the Black Dog watched them, sitting under the trees, grinning.

All the little rat dogs of the village hid under the huts.

"Soon we will raid Hoa again!" shouted young Gim. "We will follow the Spirit Dog to victory!"

"You will follow me," said the war chief, Yu.

"You will follow our advice," said the oldest man, Imfa.

The women kept the mead jars filled so the men could get drunk, but stayed away from the victory dance, as always. They met together and talked in the starlight by the drying racks.

When the men were all lying around drunk, the two Hoa women who had been captured tried to creep away in the darkness; but the Black Dog stood before them, baring its teeth and growling. They turned back, frightened.

Some of the village women came from the drying racks to meet them, and they began to talk together. The women of the Farim and the Hoa speak the women's language, which is the same in both tribes, though the men's language is not.

"Where did this kind of dog come from?" asked Imfa's Wife.

"We do not know," the older Hoa woman said. "When our men went out to raid, it appeared running before them, and attacked your warriors. And a second time it did that. So the old men in our village have been feeding it with venison and live coneys and rat dogs, calling it the Victory Spirit. Today it turned on us and gave your men the victory."

"We too can feed the dog," said Imfa's Wife. And the women discussed this for a while.

Yu's Aunt went back to the drying racks and took from them a whole shoulder of dried smoked venison. Imfa's Wife smeared some paste on the meat. Then Yu's Aunt carried it towards the Black Dog. "Here, doggy," she said. She dropped it on the ground. The Black Dog came forward snarling, snatched the piece of meat, and began tearing at it.

"Good doggy," said Yu's Aunt.

Then all the women went to their huts. Yu's Aunt took the captives into her hut and gave them sleeping mats and coverlets.

In the morning the warriors of Farim awoke with aching heads and bodies. They saw and heard the children of Farim, all in a group, chattering like little birds. What were they looking at?

The body of the Black Dog, stiff and stark, pierced through and through with a hundred fishing spears.

"The women have done this thing," said the warriors.

"With poisoned meat and fishing spears," said Yu's Aunt.

"We did not advise you to do this thing," said the old men.

"Nevertheless," said Imfa's Wife, "it is done."

Ever thereafter the Farim raided the Hoa and the Hoa raided the Farim at reasonable intervals, and they fought to the death on the traditional and customary battlefields and came home victorious with their dead, who watched the warriors dance the victory dance, and were satisfied.

THE WAR ACROSS THE ALON

In ancient days in Mahigul, two city-states, Meyun and Huy, were rivals in commerce and learning and the arts, and also quarreled continually over the border between their pasturelands.

The myth of the founding of Meyun went thus: the goddess Tarv, having spent a particularly pleasant night with a young mortal, a cowherd named Mey, gave him her blue starry mantle. She told him that when he spread it out, all the ground it covered would be the site of a great city, of which he would be lord. It seemed to Mey that his city would be rather a small one, maybe five feet long and three feet wide; but he picked a nice bit of his father's pastureland and spread the goddess's mantle on the grass. And behold, the mantle spread and spread, and the more he unfolded it the more there was to unfold, until it covered all the hilly land between two streams, the little Unon and the larger Alon. Once he got the border marked, the starry mantle ascended to its owner. An enterprising cowherd, Mey got a city going and ruled it long and well; and after his death it went on thriving.

As for Huy, its myth was this: a maiden named Hu slept out in her father's plow lands one warm summer night. The god Bult looked down, saw her, and more or less automatically ravished her. Hu was enraged. She did not accept his droit du seigneur. She announced she was going to go tell his wife. To placate her the god told her she would bear him a hundred sons, who would found a great city on the very spot where she had lost her virginity. On finding that she was more pregnant than seemed possible, Hu was angrier than ever and went straight to Bult's wife, the goddess Tarv. Tarv could not undo what Bult had done, but she could alter things a bit. In due time Hu bore a hundred daughters. They became enterprising young women, who founded a city on their maternal grandfather's farm and ruled it long and well; and after they died, it went on thriving.

Unfortunately, part of the western boundary line of Hu's father's farm ran in a curve that crossed the stream to which the eastern edge of Tarv's starry cloak had reached.

After a generation of disputing about who owned this crescent of land, which at its widest reached about a half mile west of the stream, the descendants of Mey and Hu took their claims to their source, the goddess Tarv and her husband Bult. But the divine couple could not agree on a settlement, or indeed on anything else.

Bult backed the Huyans and would hear no arguments. He had told Hu her descendants would own the land and rule the city, and that was that, even if they had all turned out girls.

Tarv, who had some sense of fair play but did not feel any great warmth towards the swarming progeny of her husband's hundred bastard daughters, said that she'd lent Mey her mantle before Bult raped Hu, so Mey had prior claim to the land, and that was that.

Bult consulted some of his granddaughters, who pointed out that that piece of land west of the river had been part of Hu's father's family farm for at least a century before Tarv lent her mantle to Mey. No doubt, said the granddaughters, the slight extension of the mantle onto Hu's father's land had been a mere oversight, which the City of Huy would be willing to overlook, provided the City of Meyun paid a small reparation of sixty bullocks and ten thubes of gold. One of the thubes of gold would be pounded into gold leaf to cover the altar of the Temple of Mighty Bult in the City of Huy. And that would be the end of it.

Tarv consulted no one. She said that when she said the city's land would be all that her mantle covered, she meant exactly that, no more, no less. If the people of Meyun wanted to coat the altar of Starry Tarv in their city with gold leaf (which they had already done), that was fine, but it had no effect on her decision, which was based on unalterable fact and inspired by divine justice.

It was at this point that the two cities took up arms; and from this time on Bult and Tarv played no recorded role in events, however constantly and fervently invoked by their descendants and devotees in Meyun and Huy.

For the next couple of generations the dispute simmered, sometimes breaking out in armed forays from Huy across the stream to the land they claimed on its western bank. About a mile and a half of the length of the stream was in dispute. The Alon was some thirty yards wide at its shallowest, narrower where it ran between banks five feet high. There were some good trout pools in the northern end of the disputed reach.

The forays from Huy always met fierce resistance from Meyun. Whenever the Huyans succeeded in keeping the piece of land west of the Alon, they put up a wall around it in a semicircle out from the stream and back. The men of Meyun would then gather their forces, lead a foray against the wall, drive the Huyans back across the Alon, pull the Huyans' wall down, and erect a wall running along the east side of the stream for a mile and a half.

But that was the part of the stream to which the Huyan herders were accustomed to drive their cattle to drink. They would immediately begin pulling down the Meyunian wall. Archers of Meyun shot at them, hitting sometimes a man, sometimes a cow. The rage of Huy boiled over, and another foray burst forth from the gates of the city and retook the land west of the Alon. Peacemakers intervened. The Council of the Fathers of Meyun met in conclave, the Council of the Mothers of Huy met in conclave, they ordered the combatants to withdraw, sent messengers and diplomats back and forth across the Alon, tried to reach a settlement, and failed. Or sometimes they succeeded, but then a cowherd of Huy would take his cattle across the stream into the rich pastures where since time immemorial they had grazed, and cowherds of Meyun would round up the trespassing herds and drive them to the walled paddocks of their city, and the cowherd of Huy would rush home vowing to bring down the wrath of Bult upon the thieves and get his cattle back. Or two fishermen fishing the quiet pools of the Alon above the cattle crossing would quarrel over whose pools they were fishing, and stride back to their respective cities vowing to keep poachers out of their waters. And it would all start up again.

Not a great many were killed in these forays, but still they caused a fairly steady mortality among the young men of both cities. At last the Councilwomen of Huy decided that this running sore must be healed once for all, and without bloodshed. As so often, invention was the mother of discovery. Copper miners of Huy had recently developed a powerful explosive. The Councilwomen saw in it the means to end the war.

They ordered out a large workforce. Guarded by archers and spearmen, these Huyans, by furious digging and the planting of explosive charges in the ground, in the course of twenty-six hours changed the course of the Alon for the whole disputed mile and a half. With their explosives they dammed the stream and dug a channel that led it to run in an arc along the border they claimed, west of its old course. This new course followed the line of ruins of the various walls they had built and Meyun had torn down.

They then sent messengers across the meadows to Meyun to announce, in polite and ceremonious terms, that peace between the cities was restored, since the boundary Meyun had always claimed—the east bank of the river Alon—was acceptable to Huy, so long as the cattle of Huy were allowed to drink at certain watering places on the eastern bank.

A good part of the Council of Meyun was willing to accept this solution. They admitted that the wily women of Huy were bilking them out of their property; but it was only a bit of pastureland not two miles long and less than a half mile wide; and their fishing rights to the pools of the Alon were no longer to be in question. They urged acceptance of the new course of the river. But sterner minds refused to yield to chicanery. The Lactor General made a speech in which he cried that every inch of that precious soil was drenched in the red blood of the sons of Mey and made sacred by the starry cloak of Tarv. That speech turned the vote.

Meyun had not yet invented very effective explosives, but it is easier to restore a stream to its natural course than to induce it to follow an artificial one. A wildly enthusiastic workforce of citizens, digging furiously, guarded by archers and spearmen, returned the Alon to its bed in the course of a single night.

There was no resistance, no bloodshed, for the Council of Huy, bent on peace, had forbidden their guards to attack the party from Meyun. Standing on the east bank of the Alon, having met no opposition, smelling victory in the air, the Lactor General cried, "Forward, men! Crush the conniving strumpets once and for all!" And with one cry, says the annalist, all the archers and spearmen of Meyun, followed by many of the citizens who had come to help move the river back to its bed, rushed across the half mile of meadow to the walls of Huy.

They broke into the city, but the city guards were ready for them, as were the citizens, who fought like tigers to defend their homes. When, after an hour's bloody fighting, the Lactor General was slain—felled by a forty-pint butter churn shoved out a window onto his head by an enraged housewife—the forces of Meyun retreated in disorder back to the Alon. They regrouped and defended the stream bravely until nightfall, when they were driven back across it and took refuge within their own city walls. The guards and citizens of Huy did not try to enter Meyun, but went back and planted explosives and dug all night to restore the Alon to its new, west-curving course.

Given the highly infectious nature of technologies of destruction, it was inevitable that Meyun should discover how to make explosives as powerful as those of their rival. What was perhaps unusual was that neither city chose to use them as a weapon. As soon as Meyun had the explosives, their army, led by a man in the newly created rank of Sapper General, marched out and blew up the dam across the old bed of the Alon. The river rushed into its former course, and the army marched back to Meyun.

Under their new Supreme Engineer, appointed by the disappointed and vindictive Councilwomen of Huy, the guards marched out and did some sophisticated dynamiting which, by blocking the old course and deepening the access to the new course of the river, led the Alon to flow happily back into the latter.

Henceforth the territorialism of the two city-states was expressed almost entirely in explosions. Though many soldiers and citizens and a great many cows were killed, as technological improvements led to ever more powerful agents of destruction which could blow up ever larger quantities of earth, these charges were never planted as mines with the intention of killing. Their sole purpose was to fulfill the great aim of Meyun and Huy: to change the course of the river.

For nearly a hundred years the two city-states devoted the greatest part of their energies and resources to this purpose.

By the end of the century, the landscape of the region had been enormously and irrevocably altered. Once green meadows had sloped gently down to the willow-clad banks of the little Alon with its clear trout pools, its rocky narrows, its muddy watering places and cattle crossings where cows stood dreaming udder-deep in the cool shallows. In place of this there was now a canyon, a vast chasm, half a mile across from lip to lip and nearly two thousand feet deep. Its overhanging walls were of raw earth and shattered rock. Nothing could grow on them; even when not destabilised by repeated explosions, they eroded in the winter rains, slipping down continually in rockfalls and land-slides that blocked the course of the brown, silt-choked torrent at the bottom, forcing it to undercut the walls on the other side, causing more slides and erosion, which kept widening and lengthening the canyon.

Both the cities of Meyun and Huy now stood only a few hundred yards from the edge of a precipice. They hurled defi-ance at each other across the abyss which had eaten up their pas-tures, their fields, their cattle, and all their thubes of gold.

As the river and all the disputed land was now down at the bottom of this huge desolation of mud and rock, there was noth-ing to be gained by blowing it up again; but habit is powerful.

The war did not end until the dreadful night when in a sud-den, monstrous moment, half the city of Meyun shivered, tilted, and slid bodily into the Grand Canyon of the Alon.

The charges which destabilised the east wall of the canyon had been set, not by the Supreme Engineer of Huy, but by the Sapper General of Meyun. To the ravaged and terrified people of Meyun, the disaster was still not their fault, but Huy's fault: it was because Huy existed that the Sapper General had set his mis-placed charges. But many citizens of Huy came hurrying across the Alon, crossing it miles to the north or south where the canyon was shallower, to help the survivors of the enormous mudslide which had swallowed half Meyun's houses and inhabitants.

Their honest generosity was not without effect. A truce was declared. It held, and was made into a peace.

Since then the rivalry between Meyun and Huy has been intense but nonexplosive. Having no more cows or pastures, they live off tourists. Perched on the very brink of the West Rim of the Grand Canyon, what is left of Meyun has the advantage of a dramatic and picturesque site, which attracts thousands of visitors every year. But most of the visitors actually stay in Huy, where the food is better, and which is only a very short stroll from the East Rim with its marvelous views of the canyon and the half-buried ruins of Old Meyun.

Each city maintains on its respective side a winding path for tourists riding donkeys to descend among the crags and strange, towering mud formations of the canyon to the little River Alon that flows, clear again, though cowless and troutless, in the depths. There the tourists have a picnic on the grassy banks. The guides from Huy tell their tourists the amusing legend of the Hundred Daughters of Bult, and the guides from Meyun tell their tourists the entertaining myth of the Starry Cloak of Tarv. Then they all ride their donkeys slowly back up to the light.

Great Joy

I learned recently that there is a restricted plane. It came as a shock. I'd taken it for granted that once you got the hang of Sita Dulip's Method, you could go from any airport to any plane, and that the options were essentially infinite. The frequent updates to the *Encyclopedia Planaria* are evidence that the number of known planes keeps increasing. And I thought all of them were accessible (under the right conditions) from all the others, until my cousin Sulie told me about The Holiday Plane™.

This plane can be reached only from certain airports, all of them in the United States, most of them in Texas. At Dallas and Houston there are Holiday Plane Club Lounges for tour groups to this special destination. How they induce the necessary stress and indigestion in these lounges, I do not really want to know.

Nor do I have any wish to visit the plane; but Cousin Sulie has been going there for several years. She was on the way there when she told me about it, and in response to my request she kindly brought me back a whole tote bag full of flyers, brochures, and promotional materials, from which I compiled this description. There is a Web site, though its address seems to change without notice.

Any history of the place has to be mere guesswork. Going by the dates on the brochures, it is not more than ten years old. I imagine a scenario of its origin: a bunch of businessmen are delayed at a Texas airport, and get to talking in that bar where first-class and business-class persons can go but other persons cannot. One of the businessmen suggests they all try out Sita Dulip's Method. Through inexperience or bravado they find themselves not on one of the popular tourist planes but on one not even listed in Rornan's *Handy Guide*. And they find it, in their view, virgin: unexplored, undeveloped, a Third World plane just waiting for the wizardry of the entrepreneur, the magic touch of exploitation.

I imagine that the native population was spread out over many small islands and that they were very poor, or fatally hospitable, or both. Evidently they were ready and willing, through innocent hope of gain or love of novelty, to adopt a new way of life. At any rate, ready or not, they learned to do what they were told to do and behave the way they were taught to behave by the Great Joy Corporation.

Great Joy has a kind of Chinese sound to it, but all the promotional literature Cousin Sulie brought me was printed in the United States. The Great Joy Corporation owns the trademarked name of the plane and issues the PR. Beyond that, I know nothing about Great Joy. I have not tried to investigate it. It's no use. There is no information about corporations. There is only disinformation. Even after they collapse, imploding into a cratered ruin stinking of burnt stockholder and surrounded by an impenetrable barrier formed by members of Congress and other government officials holding hands and wearing yellow tape marked Private Property, No Trespassing, Keep Out, No Hunting, Fishing, or Accounting—even then there is no truth in them.

Insofar as one can trust the promotional copy, the world of Great Joy is mostly a warm, shallow ocean dotted with small islands. They look flatter than our volcanic Pacific islands, more like big sandbars. The climate is said to be warm and pleasant. There must be, or must have been, native plants and animals, but there is nothing about them in the advertising. The only trees in the photographs are firs and coconut palms in large pots. There is nothing about the people, either, unless you count references to "the friendly, colorful natives."

The largest island, or anyhow the one with by far the most elaborate advertising copy, is Christmas Island.

That is where Cousin Sulie goes every time she gets the chance. Since she lives in rural South Carolina and has a daughter in San Diego and a son in Minneapolis, she gets the chance fairly often, so long as she makes sure to change planes at the right places: the major Texas airports, Denver, and Salt Lake City. Her son and daughter expect her to visit them sometime in August, because that's when she likes to do her Christmas shopping, and again perhaps in early December, when she panics about things she didn't buy in August.

"I just get right into the spirit just *thinking* about Christmas

Island!" she says. "Oh, it is just such a *happy* place! And the prices are really just as low as Wal-Mart, and a much better selection."

Mild and sunny as the climate is said to be, all the windows of the shops and stores in Noël City, Yuleville, and O Little Town are rimed with frost, the sills heaped with eternal snow, the frames garlanded with fir and holly. Bells ring continuous peals from dozens of spires and steeples. Cousin Sulie says there are no churches under the steeples, only retail space, but the steeples are very picturesque. All the retail spaces and the crowded streets are full of the sound of carols wafting endlessly over the heads of the Christmas shoppers and the natives. The natives in the photographs are dressed in approximately Victorian costume, the men with tailcoats and top hats, the women with crinolines. The boys carry hoops, the girls rag dolls. The natives fill up the spaces in the streets, hurrying merrily about, making sure there are no empty blocks or unbustling squares. They drive sightseers about in horse-drawn carriages and char-a-bancs, sell bunches of mistletoe, and sweep crossings. Cousin Sulie says they always speak to you so nicely. I asked what they said. They say, "Merry Christmas!" or "A fine evening to you!" or *"Gahbressa sebberwun!"* She was not sure what this last phrase meant, but when she repeated it as she had heard it, I identified it, I think.

It is Christmas Eve all year long on Christmas Island, and all the shops and stores of Noël City and Yuleville, 220 of them according to the brochure, are open 24/7/365.

"Those little tacky Christmas-All-Year-Round-type shops like we have at home," Sulie says, "they're just nowhere. I mean to tell you. Why, there's one store in Noël City that is *entirely bags*. You know, pretty paper bags? or foil or cellophane? for gifts you haven't got the time to wrap, or they're kind of knobbly? So you just pop them in a bag with some of that curly foamy-like paper ribbon spilling out, and it is as pretty as it could be and just as good next year, too, if you fold it nice."

When she has done her shopping and visited the Angels Nook, a sort of chapel where tea is served in the Little Drummer Boy Inn where she stays—the Adeste Fideles Inn, she says, is very nice but just too expensive—Sulie treats herself with a trip to O Little Town. She says O Little Town is her "favorite place in the world."

If she has time, she goes there by one-horse sleigh, over the Christmas Tree Mile, a road lined with decorated fir trees in large pots and kept covered with artificial snow, the natural variety not being available. Cousin Sulie is vague about the landscape beyond the fir trees. "Oh just sandy, like pine barrens, I guess," she says, "only no pines. But you should hear those bells just jingling! And do you know that horse always has a bobtail? Just like in the song?"

If her time is limited, she goes from Noël City to O Little Town on the Xmas Xpress, a jet trolley. In O Little Town one must walk, or if unable or disinclined to walk, one may ride the open-sided Santa Trains, operated by elves, which circulate constantly among all the points of interest.

"You can't get lost," says Cousin Sulie, "and you know, it's so *safe*. Just think of the difference from all that ugliness in the Holy Land? Feeling safe just makes such a difference."

There are churches as well as steeples in O Little Town; they

are replicas of famous sites in Jerusalem, Rome, Guadalupe, Atlanta, and Salt Lake City. Villagers dressed in what my cousin calls "sort of Bible clothes" keep stalls in a lively marketplace selling peppermint canes and ribbon candy, toys, craft items, and souvenirs; children tumble in the dooryards of little cottages; now and then a shepherd drives a small flock of sheep down the street. Just outside the village is what the brochures describe in vibrant and reverential language as the high point of every visit: the Manger.

Cousin Sulie gets a little teary when she talks about it. "It seems like outside, because you go into like a big tent. Like a circus, you know? but more like a what do you call them? A planetarium? A planetarium. With black night sky, and *stars* overhead? Even when it's a sunny day outside. It's the night and the stars, there. And the Star, the Christmas Star. Just blazing there right over that poor humble little manger. Oh, it just puts our First Baptist lawn scene to shame. I am here to tell you. It is so beautiful. And the animals. Not just a sheep or two, but *flock*s of sheep, and cows, and donkeys, and the camels, and they're *real*. And the people are real! Alive. And that adorable baby! Oh, I know they must just be actors and do it for a living, but I do feel they must be blessed by it even if they don't know it. I spoke to one of the Josephs once, I recognised him in the yard of one of those sweet little cottages in the village. I'd seen him being Joseph more than once, a fine-looking man, about fifty, he has a nice face, and you know somehow Joseph isn't so awesome as the others? The Kings, now, I'd never. And that little Mary is just too angelic for this world. But Joseph seems like more approachable. So I greeted him, and he smiled and waved his hands like foreigners do and said *Merra-Krissma!* the way they do. They're just all so sweet. They truly show the Christmas spirit."

Sulie told me that she feels it a great pity sick children cannot be taken to Christmas Island. "Poor little mites who just can't wait those months till Santa comes—if they could only see Santa's Ride in Yuleville! It's every evening at nine and again at eleven. Those reindeer come a-clattering over the rooftop of the Cozy Home, you can see it from the Town Square or on the closed-circuit TV, and Santa gets out of the sleigh and just pops down that chimney like a jack-in-the-box backward—wouldn't they love to see that? And Rudolph's nose just glowing like a taillight! But it seems like there's no way they can figure out how to bring the children there without causing them too much distress. Even though the tour has scientifically perfected the transition for adults. You know, I wouldn't go to just any of those planes. Heaven only knows where you might end up! Christmas Island is a guaranteed destination. But it is a pity. You can't just take a poor little sick child to suffer and worry in a busy airport even though it would be such a treat for them." And tenderhearted Sulie sighs. "I don't deserve it," she says. "Sometimes, you know, I think I won't go back there again? I shouldn't. It's greedy. I should just wait for Christmas to come to me. But it's so long between Decembers..."

There are other holiday isles on the Great Joy Corporation plane. Cousin Sulie has visited only Easter Island. She didn't like it much, perhaps because she had a cold coming on and was worried about her flight out of Denver to Seattle. She had, rather riskily, changed planes while actually sitting in the plane while it was sitting on the ground being de-iced for the third time in a snowstorm. "It just wasn't a very good time to travel," she said.

The cover of the brochure shows a sand dune crowned with a row of the familiar frowning monoliths of the South Sea Easter Island. My cousin seems to have missed these or ignored them. "I guess I was looking for something a little more on the sacred side?" she said. "I did enjoy the display of those Russian Emperors' eggs. The rubies and gold and all. They were pretty. But you wonder why emperors need so many eggs. They kept them on their feet, I read somewhere. It seems strange. I suppose they were Communists. But the rabbits? Sakes! Rabbits just everywhere. Underfoot. I never much liked rabbits since James tried raising rabbits to sell to butcher markets, down in Augusta, Fred Ingley talked him into it, but there wasn't hardly any market for them, and then James got his tumor, and the rabbits took some rabbit disease and died all in a week, just died like flies, every last one of them, and I had no way to get rid of all that miserable mess but set fire to those hutch things and burn them to the ground. Oh, my. I don't like to recall that... Well, then. There's lots of little chickies peeping around, they're sweet. And the baskets in the Bunny Hop Market are just gorgeous. But I couldn't afford anything much. And it was hot! I kept thinking about that blizzard in Denver. I just wasn't in the right mood, I guess. So *many* eggs and rabbits."

To judge by the promotional materials, Christmas, Easter, and Fourth are the biggest, most developed, and most popular islands. The rather modest brochure for Hollo-Een! is all about Family Fun and clearly aimed at parents and children trapped in airports.

To judge by the photographs, Hollo-Een! Island swarms with pumpkins, I can't tell whether honest pumpkins or plastic ones. There is a fairground with roller coaster, spook rides, tunnel of horrors, etc. The natives running concessions, waiting tables, cleaning rooms, etc., are dressed as witches, ghosts, space aliens, and Ronald Reagan. There is "Trick or Treating Every Evening! Safe! Supervised! (All candy guaranteed safe and healthful)." While the children are being led about from house to house of Spook-E-Ville, the parents can watch any one of "One Hundred Horror Movies" on the big-screen TV in their suite in Addams House or Frankenstein's Castle.

I detected a slightly stuffy note in Cousin Sulie's voice when she gave me the brochure. Its text contains an inordinate number of blandly but insistently reassuring statements from Protestant ministers of various denominations. They all describe Hollo-Een! as clean, safe, wholesome family fun. Absolutely nothing "harmful" or "disturbing." But I am sure the keen noses of true believers sniff that brochure for brimstone, and their keen eyes discern, on those alien sands, the print of the cloven foot.

The promotional material for Fourth Island is far more lavish and not at all defensive. From the Permanent Living Reenactment of the Flag Raising on Iwo Jima to the Rockets' Red Glare Four-Hour Fireworks Display every night, from the United We Stand Steak House by way of the statue-lined Avenue of the Presidents to the Under God Indivisible Prayer Chapel, it is all on a grand scale, and every last piece of it is red, white, blue, striped, and starred. The Great Joy Corporation is evidently expecting or receiving patriotic visitors in great numbers. Interactive displays of the Museum of Our Heroes, the Gun Show, and the All-American Victory Gardens (salvia, lobelia, candytuft) feature large on the Web site, where one can also at all times recite the Pledge of Allegiance interactively with a chorus of five thousand virtual schoolchildren.

Accommodations on Fourth Island range from The ★★ George Washington Country Inn to The ★★★★★★ George W. Bush Grand Luxury Hotel and Suites. (It was foolish of me to hope for a grim motel with hourly rates called The Last Resort of Scoundrels.)

In comparison to the high-rises over white sand beaches, blue sea, red umbrellas, the imposing avenues, and the marble vistas of Fourth Island, Valentine's Island looks cozy and old-fashioned. It is of course heart-shaped, and Truelove Town is heart-shaped too. Lots of pink and white, lots of lace, lots of honeymoon suites, and second honeymoon suites, and eternal honeymoon suites, at the Chocolate Box Hotel. Bicycles built for two may be rented. Smiling native children dressed—barely—as cupids are photographed aiming paper arrows at smiling couples in bowers of artificial roses. "Well, I suppose if you were in the right mood, with the right person, it might be nice," says Cousin Sulie, turning over the leaflets a little disdainfully.

The brochure for New Year's Island says "all facilities brand-new." There appears to be in fact only one facility: a vast hotel. It has fourteen banquet rooms and six grand ballrooms and a golf course on the roof. The only picture taken out of doors is a view of a great open courtyard strung with Chinese lanterns. New Year's Island is evidently designed for brief visits, a few hours or a single night, by travelers who have not much time to spend and want to spend it at a party, for aside from the golf course that is all the entertainment offered—"The Party of Your Life!"

Actually a wide choice of parties: one in a gilded ballroom, with balloons and waltzes and an orchestra; one in a "Green-which Village Flapper Days Loft," with jazz and bootleg gin; one in a "Cheers-Type Bar," one at a "Sixties Hippie Love-In," and so on. An appropriate costume for the evening, from ball gown or black tie to purple mohawk wig and temporary nose and lip studs, may be rented. Studying the faces in the photographs of parties in progress, I'd guess that an appropriate companion for the evening may also be rented. Among the dancers, at the buffet tables, clinking champagne glasses, are a lot of pretty, young women and handsome, fortyish men. They are all slender, all dark, and all smiling. They don't look like tourists. The tourists do.

I got the impression from these brochures that a visit to the Great Joy Corporation's plane might be quite expensive, though no prices are listed. If you call the 800 number or try to find out on the Net, they just assure you that transportation to the plane is "absolutely free," and suggest brightly that you'll want to bring a "valid credit card." Cousin Sulie tells me that "it isn't half as bad as that place with the funny name in Florida that Sally Ann insisted on us going to. Honey, *those* people, they'll *skin* you."

On New Year's Island just before midnight (which I believe occurs every twelve hours, possibly every six) everybody who can still stand up flocks out to the great courtyard, where a three-story-tall TV screen shows the ball falling down in Times Square. Everybody holds hands and champagne glasses with the usual difficulty and sings "Auld Lang Syne." There are fireworks and more champagne, and the party goes on. And on, and on. I wonder how they clean the party rooms. Maybe they have duplicate rooms, one in use and one being cleaned. Maybe nobody notices. I wonder how they get drunks back to their airport of origin on time, and if they don't, do they get sued? Not that it's any use suing a corporation. I wonder what they give people to smoke at the Hippie Love-In Party and to use at the Punk Underground Party, and how they get *them* back where they started.

Anyhow, where it's always New Year's Eve it's never New Year's Day. No resolutions need be made. There's no need even to send the partygoers home so long as they're willing to carry on partying until the countdown begins again and the ball falls down in Times Square again and the fireworks go off again and they sing "Auld Lang Syne" again and have some more champagne. Beyond this my imagination balks. It will not furnish me with any further possibilities concerning life on New Year's Island. It informs me that there are none.

Cousin Sulie and I don't see eye to eye on everything, but in this case we agree. "I wouldn't go to that party island," she said. "I always did *hate* New Year's Eve."

I noticed that one element of the entertainment in the great courtyard was a Chinese New Year in San Francisco Dragon Parade. The natives in the picture look far more convincing as Chinese Americans than as cupids or elves or Revolutionary soldiers crossing the Delaware. It got me to wondering if there were any, as it were, un-American islands on the Great Joy Corporation plane. Sulie was vague about this. "There's lots of islands," she said. "Some of them might be foreign."

With this and other questions in mind, I called my friend Sita Dulip. To my surprise, she had not even heard about the plane. I told her what I could and sent her all the literature I had.

After a week or two she called me back. She had tried to contact the Great Joy Corporation and had the expectable difficulty getting anywhere behind the 800 number. But Sita is knowledgeable and persistent, and she finally sweet-talked her way to somebody in Public Relations, who sent her a set of literature and fliers, much the same as those Sulie had collected, and also a list of memos on Island Projects. These had been generated by the PR and Development departments and were apparently under consideration by the decision makers of the corporation. They included:

Isla Cinco de Mayo (a fully developed plan that is evidently about to be implemented)

Sit Seder Every Night! (lack of detailed information on this indicates that the project has been shelved)

Kwanzaa! Afric-Island (a rough sketch of facilities and "participatory entertainments," with approving notations from higher-ups, such as *Go for it*)

Têt Everlasting (almost no details)

Holi Holi Holi (a long, enthusiastic memo, describing all the possibilities of colored water and colored powder and

classical Indian dance, signed R. Chandranathan, which
does not seem to have received encouragement from above)

Sita continues to investigate the Great Joy Corporation and
its plane.

Having written this much, I decided to put the piece away until
I had heard from Sita again. It was nearly a year before she got in
touch and brought me up to date.

Soon after we talked, Sita decided to notify the Interplanary
Agency of the operations of the Great Joy Corporation on "The
Holiday Plane™"—which turned out to have been known for
centuries to the Agency. It is described (in its original state) and
listed in the *Encyclopedia Planaria* as Musu Sum.

The Agency, as may be imagined, is overloaded with the
tasks of registering and investigating newly discovered planes, in-
stalling and inspecting transfer points, hostels, and tourist facilities, regulating interplanar relations, and a thousand such
responsibilities. But when they learned that a plane had been
closed to free entry and exit and was being operated as a sort of
prison camp for its inhabitants to the profit of the operators,
they acted at once, decisively.

I do not know how the Agency exerts its authority, or even
on what its authority rests, or what instruments of persuasion it
may use; but the Great Joy Corporation no longer exists. It has
ceased to be, as mysteriously as it came to be, still without a history, or a face, or a shred of accountability.

Sita sent me the new literature from Musu Sum. The island

resorts are now being operated by the islanders themselves as a cooperative venture, supervised for the first year by expert advisers from the Agency.

This makes sense, in that the modest subsistence economy of the region was completely destroyed by the Great Joy Corporation and cannot be restored overnight, while all the hotels and restaurants and roller coasters are in place, and people who have been trained to serve and entertain the tourists might as well use and profit by their training. On the other hand, it boggles the mind a bit. Especially Fourth Island. An orgiastic monument of American sentimental nationalism operated entirely by people who know nothing about the United States except that they were ruthlessly used by Americans for years? Well, I suppose it is not wholly improbable even on this plane. Exploitation can cut two ways.

I have met a native of Musu Sum, one of the first to take advantage of his people's newly regained freedom to travel; Sita asked him to come by and see me. He thanked me most graciously for my part in the liberation of his people. That it was a totally accidental and tangential part made no difference to Esmo So Mu. He gave me as a "gift of the gratitude of my people" a little wickerwork ball, a child's toy, rather crudely made. "We don't make such beautiful things like Americans," he said apologetically, but I think he saw that I was touched by the gift.

His English was quite fluent. He had been one of Santa's elves as a boy and then was transferred to New Year's Island as a waiter and part-time gigolo. "It was not so bad," he said, then, "It was bad," and then, his high-cheek-boned, expressive face crinkling into a laugh, "but not very-very bad. Only the food was very-very bad."

Esmo So Mu described his world: hundreds of islands, many with a population of only a family or two, scattered out over the ocean "forever." People traveled from island to island in catamarans. "Everybody go visit all the time," he said.

The Great Joy Corporation had concentrated population in one archipelago and forbidden sailing in or out of that area. "Burn boats," Esmo So Mu said briefly.

He had been born on an island south of the Holiday Islands and was now living there again. "Lots more money if I stay to work at the hotel," he said, "but I don't care." I asked him to tell me about his home. "Oh," he said, and laughed again. "You know what? In my home there's no holidays! Because we are *so* lazy! We work one, two hours, in the gardens, then we don't work. We play, we play with the children. We go sail. We fish. We swim. We sleep. We cook. We eat. We sleep. Why do we want a holiday?"

But Cousin Sulie was disappointed to find that the management has changed. "I don't expect I'll go back this August," she told me rather sadly, when I called to wish her a happy birthday. "It just doesn't seem like it would be like Christmas if it was a different nationality. Do you think?"

Wake Island

⌒

People who sleep only two or three hours in the twenty-four are always geniuses. The ones you hear about, anyway. Never mind if the ones you don't hear about are dolts. Insomnia is genius. It must be. Think of all the work you could do, the thoughts you could think, the books you could read, the love you could make, while the dull clods lie snoring.

On the plane of the Orichi, which is in many ways very similar to ours, there are people who don't sleep at all.

A group of scientists in the Orichi nation of Hy Brisal became convinced that sleep was a vestigial behavior pattern appropriate to lower mammals but not to sapient humans. Sleep might serve to keep vulnerable simians quiet and out of harm's way at night, but is as irrelevant to civilised life as hibernation would be. Worse, it is an impediment to intelligence—a recurrent damper on the brain. By interrupting the brain's ongoing functions every night, by grossly interfering with coherent thought, sleep prevents the human mind from attaining its maximum potential. *Sleep makes us stupid,* was the motto of the Orichi scientists.

Their government, fearing invasion from the rival nation of Nuum, encouraged any experimentation that might give Hy Brisal the edge in weaponry or brainpower. So, well funded, working with brilliant genetic engineers, and provided with ten patriotic pairs of fertile volunteers, all housed in a closed-gate compound, these scientists began a program, nicknamed Supersmarts by the national news net, which eagerly supported it. And in four years the first entirely sleepless babies were born. (Millions of bleary-eyed young parents might dispute that statement; but the usual baby does go to sleep, after all, just about the time its parents have to get up.)

The first Supersmart babies, however, died. Some died in their first weeks, some after several months. They cried day and night until they wasted away into silence and death.

The scientists decided that infant sleep is an extension of the fetal development process that cannot safely be bypassed.

Hy Brisal and Nuum were in a particularly confrontational phase. Rumor had it that Nuum was working on an airborne germ that would sterilise all Hy Brisalian males. Popular support for the Supersmarts program had been shaken by the loss of the infants, but the government did not waver; they sent the genetic engineers back to the drawing board and asked for a new set of volunteers. Twenty-two patriotic couples signed up on the first day. In less than two years they began to produce the new generation of Supersmarts.

The programming was delicate and accurate. The newborns would sleep as much as ordinary infants to begin with, but would gradually begin to stay awake for longer and longer periods, until by the age of four they were expected to do without sleep altogether.

And so they did. They did not waste away; they thrived. They were fine, healthy babies, all twenty-two of them. They stared up at their mothers and smiled. They kicked and cooed and sucked and crawled and did what babies do, including sleep. They were bright, because much attention was paid to them and their learning environment was rich, but they were not geniuses, yet. They learned what babies learn, including googoo and gaga, and then mama and papa, and NO, and the rest of the toddler vocabulary, at only slightly better than the average rate. Radical acceleration of learning and increase in active intelligence would come as they began staying awake.

By the time they were two, most of them were sleeping less than six hours a night. There was some natural variation in what the directors of the program called their asomnic development. The prizewinner was Baby Ha Dab, who gave up naps at ten months, and at twenty-six months was sleeping only two or three hours a night.

For several months Ha Dab, a pretty little fellow with big eyes and silvery, curly hair, was the darling of the Hy Brisalian media. He was on everybody's homescreen—"Smartsyboy." Here was Ha Dab lurching cheerily across a room to greet the Scientist General, Doctor Master Professor Uy Tug, author of

Asomnia: The Answer, who stooped with a pinched though genuine smile to shake his tiny hand. Here was Ha Dab rolling in the grass with the blapdog puppy presented to him by the Supreme Pinnacular of Hy Brisal. Here was Ha Dab cuddling down in his little bed as if to sleep, thumb in mouth, but popping up again bright-eyed to mug at the cam man. Then Smartsyboy faded from the net, as all fads fade. For over a year little was heard about the Supersmarts program.

The Hy-Brisalian Highly Intellectual Net Locus then ran a noninteractive informational video which—carefully—raised some questions concerning the validity of asomnist theory and the supersmartness of the Supersmarts test children. The most telling part of the presentation was a brief scene of Ha Dab, now three and a half and fully asomnic, playing with his blapdog. They were both charming little creatures, having a wonderful time roughhousing in the compound park, but it was rather troubling to see that the naked child followed the dog around instead of the dog following the child. Ha Dab also seemed curiously indifferent to the presence of strangers. When asked questions, he sometimes ignored the speaker and sometimes responded at random, as if neither speech nor human relationship meant much to him. Asked "Are you in school now?," he wandered off a few steps and squatted down right before the cameras to defecate. There seemed to be nothing defiant about his action. It was purely shameless.

Another child shown in the presentation, however, Ra Gna, a delicate girl of nearly four who had been designated as "slow to develop" because she was still sleeping four hours a night, responded with adorable verve to the reporters, telling them that she liked school because there were micoscopes wif wiggly fings inside of them, and that she could read her affabet book nearly. Ra Gna, however, did not become the next media darling. The Supersmarts program refused to allow any more cam men on the premises for over two years—until public curiosity and media pressure became too strong for them to withstand.

At this point Dr. Mr. Prof. Uy Tug announced that the Asomnia Test was successful. None of the twenty-two children, now just under four to just over six, was sleeping more than half an hour a night, and all were in excellent health. As for their intellectual development, he explained that since it was of course not proceeding as that of hypersomnic children did, it could not be measured by the same standards. There was, however, no possible doubt of their very high intelligence.

This did not quite satisfy the homescreen audience, or the maverick scientists who had questioned the theory of asomnism, or even the government which was supporting Dr. Mr. Prof. Uy Tug's program in hopes of a generation of geniuses who would bring Nuum to its knees and confirm Hy Brisal as the supermost superpower in the world. After a good deal of time and pressure and committee meetings, a Committee of Scientific Investigation charged with making a disinterested report was forced upon the fiercely resistant Dr. Mr. Prof. Uy Tug and his staff.

The investigators found many of the parents of the Supersmarts pathetically eager to talk to them, begging for advice, help, treatment for their children. One after another, these loving and desperate mothers and fathers said the same words: "They're sleepwalking."

One young mother, uneducated but observant, set her little

boy down in front of a mirror and told the investigator to watch him. "Mi Min," she said to the child, "look, Mi Min, who's that in the mirror? Who's that, honey? That little boy, what's he doing?" But the child "did not relate in any way to the image," as the investigator wrote. "He showed no interest in it. He never looked into the eyes of the mirror image. Later I noticed that though his glance sometimes crossed mine at random, he did not look into my eyes, nor could I look into his. I found this curiously disquieting."

The same investigator was also disturbed by the fact that none of the children pointed at anything or followed the direction of a pointing finger. "Animals and young infants," he wrote, "look at the finger rather than at the direction pointed at, and do not point themselves. Pointing as a meaningful and understood gesture is a normal spontaneous development occurring in an infant's first year."

The Supersmarts obeyed direct, simple orders, erratically. If told, "Go to the kitchen," or "Sit down," they often did so. If asked "Are you hungry?," a child might or might not go to the kitchen or to the table to receive food. When hurt, none of the children would run to an adult crying about the "owie." They just crouched down, whimpering or silent. A father said, "It's like he doesn't know it happened to him, like something happened but he doesn't know it happened to him." He added proudly, "He's tough. A real soldier. Never asks for help."

Spoken endearments seemed to mean nothing to the children, though if offered a physical embrace they might nuzzle or cuddle up to the speaker. Sometimes a child would say or hum endearments—"Nice nice nice," "Mama soft, mama soft"—but not in response to loving words from the parent. They responded to their names, and most of them if asked their name would say it, though some did not. The parents reported that they increasingly seemed to "just talk to themselves" or "just don't listen" and that their use of pronouns was often arbitrary—"you" for "I," or "me" for "them." All their speech seemed to be increasingly spontaneous not responsive, random not purposive.

After over a year of patient and intensive study and discussion, the investigators published their report. Its language was very cautious. They put a good deal of emphasis on the case of Ra Gna, who had continued to sleep up to an hour a night and even occasionally to doze off in the daytime, and was thus considered, in terms of the experiment, a failure. Ra Gna's difference from the other Supersmarts was vividly and unguardedly described by one of the investigators to a homescreen reporter: "She's a sweet kid, dreamy. They're all dreamy. She wanders off, I mean her mind does; talking to her is kind of like talking to the dog, you know? She sort of listens, but most of it's just noise to her. But sometimes she sort of shivers like somebody waking up, and then she's *there,* and she *knows* it. None of the other kids ever do. They aren't there. They aren't anywhere."

The conclusion of the investigators was that "permanent wakefulness appears to prevent the brain from achieving full consciousness."

The media screamed with gusto for a month about Zombie Tots—the Waking Brain-Dead—Programmed Autism—Infant Sacrifice on Altar of Science—"Why Won't They Let Me Sleep, Mommy?"—and then lost interest.

The government's interest was kept alive for twelve more

years by the unflagging persuasion of Dr. Mr. Prof. Uy Tug, who had firm allies in one of the Supreme Pinnacular's most valued advisers and several influential generals of the army. Then, abruptly and without public notice, funding for the project was withdrawn.

Many of the supervising scientists had left the compound already. Dr. Mr. Prof. Uy Tug suffered a heart attack and died. The distraught parents of the Supersmarts—who had been forced to stay in the compound all these years, well fed and clothed of course and with access to all modern conveniences except communicative devices—got out and yelled for help.

Their children were now fifteen to seventeen years old and entirely sleepless. With puberty, they had fully entered into the state some observers described as altered consciousness, others as waking unconsciousness, and others as sleepwalking. The last word was particularly inappropriate. They were anything but asleep. Nor were they oblivious to their surroundings, as is the sleepwalker who wanders out into traffic or tries to scrub the damn'd spot from her hands. They were physically aware at all times. They were never not aware.

Bodily they were healthy. Because they were fed well and regularly, with food always available, they had no hunting or foraging skills. They walked about, ran aimlessly, sometimes swinging on the playsets furnished them or from tree branches in the park, scratching the dirt into pits and heaps and wrestling with one another. As they matured, these puppy fights had begun to lead to sex play and soon to copulation.

Two mothers and a father had committed suicide during the long captivity, and a father had died of a stroke. The forty remaining parents had kept up a round-the-clock watch for years, trying to restrain their children: twelve adolescent girls and ten adolescent boys, all awake all the time. The conditions of the experiment prevented the parents from locking any doors; they could not keep the young people from access to one another. The parents' pleas for locks and contraceptives had been rejected by Dr. Mr. Prof. Uy Tug, who was convinced that the *second* generation of asomnics would fully vindicate his theory, as expounded in the unpublished manuscript of *Asomnia: The Answer Is to Come.*

When the compound was opened, four of the girls had had babies, which were being looked after by the grandparents. Three more of the girls were pregnant. One of the mothers had been raped by one of the asomnic boys and was also pregnant. She was permitted to abort the fetus.

There followed an obscure and shameful period in which the government disclaimed any responsibility for the experiment and left its subjects to fend for themselves. Some of the Supersmarts were exploited sexually and for pornographic purposes. One was killed by his mother, allegedly in self-defense; she served a brief term in prison. At last, under the rule of the new Forty-Fourth Supreme Pinnacular, all the surviving asomnics, including their infants, were taken to a reservation on a remote island in the vast Ru Mu River delta, where their descendants have remained ever since, wards of the nation of Hy Brisal.

The second generation failed to vindicate Uy Tug's theory but proved the skill of the genetic engineers: they bred absolutely true. No descendant of the Supersmarts has been capable of sleep after the age of five.

There are now about fifty-five asomnics on Wake Island. The climate is very warm, and they go naked. Fruit, cheese, bread, and other foods that need no preparation are left on the shore by an army jetboat every second day. Except for these provisions, tossed ashore from the boat, a strict no-contact policy is maintained. No humanitarian or medical aid is permitted. Tourists, including those from other planes, are allowed on a neighboring islet, where they can catch glimpses of the asomnics from a blind through high-power telescopes. Teams of scientific observers are occasionally lowered from helicopters into two observation towers on the island itself. These towers, inaccessible to the asomnics, are equipped with infrared and other highly sophisticated viewing devices; the observers are hidden behind one-way glass. Pickets from the Save the Asomnic Babies Association are permitted to march and keep vigils on the south shore. From time to time these SABA activists make rescue attempts by boat, but the army jetboats and helicopters have always forestalled them.

The asomnics bask, walk, run, climb, swing, wrestle, groom themselves and one another, hold and suckle babies, and have sex. Males fight in sexual rivalry and often beat females who reject intercourse. All fight occasionally over food, and there have been a number of apparently causeless killings. Group rape is common, when males are excited by seeing others copulate. There are some indications of affectional bonding between mother and infant and between siblings. Otherwise there are no social relations. No teaching occurs, and there is no sign of individuals learning skills or customs by imitation. Most of the females bear a child a year from the age of thirteen or fourteen on. Their maternal skills can only be innate, and the question of whether human beings have any innate skills has not yet been settled; in any case, most of the babies die. The mothers leave dead babies where they lie. After weaning, children fend for themselves; since an excess of food is always provided, a fair number of them survive to puberty.

Adult female death is usually from brutality or complications of childbirth. Female asomnics seldom reach thirty years. Males live longer, if they survive the dangerous late teens and early twenties when fighting is all but constant. The longest-lived inhabitant of Wake Island, FB-204, nicknamed Fibby by the observer team, was a female who lived to seventy-one. Fibby bore one infant at age fourteen and was apparently sterile thereafter. She never rejected a male's effort to copulate and so was seldom beaten. She was shy and very lazy, rarely appearing on the beach except to pick up food and retreat into the trees with it.

The current patriarch is a grizzled male, MTT-311, fifty-six years old, muscular and well-made. He spends most days basking on the sand beaches, and at night roams endlessly through the forests of the interior. Sometimes he digs holes and ditches with his hands, or piles up rocks to dam a creek, apparently for the physical pleasure of doing so, as the dams serve no purpose and are never made watertight enough to divert the stream. One of the young females spends a part of almost every night building up piles of torn bark and leaves like huge nests, though she never uses them for anything. Several females hunt for ants or grubs in fallen trees and eat them one by one. These are the only observed evidences of purposive behavior beyond the fulfillment of immediate physical needs.

Though they are extremely unclean and the females age

quickly, most asomnics are handsome in youth. All observers comment on their expression, described as bland, serene, supernally calm. A recent book about the asomnics was entitled "The Happy People"—with the Orichi equivalent of a question mark.

Orichi thinkers continue to argue about them. Are you happy if you aren't conscious of being happy? What is consciousness? Is consciousness the great boon we consider it? Which is better off, a lizard basking in the sun or a philosopher? Better off in what way and for what? There have been lizards far longer than there have been philosophers. Lizards do not bathe, do not bury their dead, and do not perform scientific experiments. There have been many more lizards than philosophers. Are lizards, then, a more successful species than philosophers? Does God love lizards better than he loves philosophers?

However one may decide such questions, observation of the asomnics, or of lizards, seems to indicate that consciousness is not necessary to living a contented sentient life. Indeed, when carried to such an extreme as human beings have carried it, consciousness may prevent true contentment: the worm in the apple of happiness. Does consciousness of being interfere with being—pervert, stunt, cripple it? It seems that every mystical practice on every plane seeks precisely to escape from consciousness. If Nirvana is the mind freed of itself, allowed to rejoin the body in the body's pure oneness with its world or god, have not the asomnics achieved Nirvana?

Certainly consciousness comes at a high cost. The price of it, evidently, is the third of our lives we spend blind, deaf, dumb, helpless, and mindless—asleep.

We do, however, dream.

The poem "Wake Island," by Nu Lap, portrays the asomnics as spending their whole life "in a dream of dreams..."

> *Dreams of waters flowing always by the sandbars*
> *dreams of bodies meeting, opening like deep flowers,*
> *dreams of eyes forever open to the sun and stars...*

A moving poem, it offers one of the very few positive views of the asomnics. But the scientists of Hy Brisal, though they might like to agree with the poet to ease their collective conscience, assert that asomnics do not and cannot dream.

As on our plane, only certain animals, including birds, dogs, cats, horses, apes, and humans, regularly enter the peculiar and highly specific brain/body condition known as sleep. Once there, and only there, some of them enter the even more peculiar state or activity, characterised by highly specific brainwave types and frequencies, called dreaming.

The asomnics lack these states of being. Their brains do not do this. They are like reptiles, who chill down into inertia but do not sleep.

A Hy Brisalian philosopher, To Had, elaborates these paradoxes: To be a self, one must also be nothing. To know oneself, one must be able to know nothing. The asomnics know the world continuously and immediately, with no empty time, no room for selfhood. Having no dreams, they tell no stories and so have no use for language. Without language, they have no lies. Thus they have no future. They live here, now, perfectly in touch. They live in pure fact. But they can't live in truth, because the way to truth, says the philosopher, is through lies and dreams.

The Nna Mmoy Language

The "garden utopia" of the Nna Mmoy deservedly enjoys the reputation of being absolutely safe—"an ideal plane for children and elderly people." The few visitors who come, including children and the aged, usually find it very dull and leave as soon as possible.

The scenery is all the same everywhere—hills, fields, parklands, woods, villages: a fertile, pretty, seasonless monotony. Cultivated land and wilderness look exactly alike. The few species of plants are all useful, yielding food or wood or fabric. There is no animal life except bacteria, some creatures resembling jellyfish in the oceans, two species of useful insect, and the Nna Mmoy.

Their manners are pleasant, but nobody has yet succeeded in talking with them.

Though their monosyllabic language is melodious to the ear, the translatomat has so much trouble with it that it cannot be relied upon even for the simplest conversation.

A look at the written language may yield some light on the problem. Written Nna Mmoy is a syllabary: each of its several thousand characters represents a syllable. Each syllable is a word, but a word with no fixed, specific meaning, only a range of possible significances determined by the syllables that come before, after, or near it. A word in Nna Mmoy has no denotation, but is a nucleus of potential connotations which may be activated, or created, by its context. Thus it would be possible to make a dictionary of Nna Mmoy only if the number of possible sentences were finite.

Texts written in Nna Mmoy are not linear, either horizontally or vertically, but radial, budding out in all directions, like tree branches or growing crystals, from a first or central word which, once the text is complete, may well be neither the center nor the beginning of the statement. Literary texts carry this polydirectional complexity to such an extreme that they resemble mazes, roses, artichokes, sunflowers, fractal patterns.

Whatever language we speak, before we begin a sentence we have an almost infinite choice of words to use. A, The, They, Whereas, Having, Then, To, Bison, Ignorant, Since, Winnemucca, In, It, As . . . *Any* word of the immense vocabulary of English may begin an English sentence. As we speak or write the sentence, each word influences the choice of the next—its syntactical function as noun, verb, adjective, etc., its person and number if a pronoun, its tense and number as a verb, etc., etc. And as the sentence goes on, the choices narrow, until the last word may very likely be the *only one* we can use. (Though a phrase, not a sentence, this quotation nicely exemplifies the point: *To be or not to—*.)

It appears that in the language of the Nna Mmoy, not only the choice of word—noun or verb, tense, person, etc.—but the meaning of each word is continuously modified by all the words that precede *or may follow* it in the sentence (if in fact the Nna Mmoy speak in sentences). And so, after receiving only a few syllables, the translatomat begins to generate a flurry of possible alternate meanings which proliferate rapidly into such a thicket of syntactical and connotational possibilities that the machine overloads and shuts down.

Purported translations of the written texts are either meaningless or ridiculously various. For example, I have come upon four different translations of the same nine-character inscription:

"All within this space are to be considered friends, as are all creatures under heaven."

"If you don't know what is inside, take care, for if you bring hatred in with you the roof will fall upon you."

"On one side of every door is mystery. Caution is useless. Friendship and enmity sink to nothing under the gaze of eternity."

"Enter boldly, stranger, and be welcome. Sit down now."

This inscription, the characters of which are written so as to form a shape like a comet with a radiant head, is often found on doors, box lids, and book covers.

The Nna Mmoy are excellent gardeners, vegetarians by necessity. Their arts are cookery, jewelry, and poetry. Each village is able to grow, gather, and make everything it needs. There is some commerce between villages, mostly involving cooked dishes, special preparations of the rather limited vegetable menu by professional cooks. Admired cooks barter their dishes for the raw materials produced by the gardeners, with a bit over. No mining has been observed, but opals, peridots, amethysts, garnets, topazes, and colored quartzes may be picked up in any stream bed; jewels are bartered for unworked or reused gold and silver. Money exists but has only a symbolic, honorary value: it is used in gambling (the Nna Mmoy play various low-keyed gambling games with dice, counters, and tiles) and to buy works of art. The money is the pearly-violet, translucent mantle, about the size and shape of a thumbnail, left by the largest species of jellyfish. Found washed up on the sea beaches, these shells are traded inland for finished jewelry and for poems—if that is what the written texts, single sheets, booklets, and scrolls, so beautiful and teasing to the eye, actually are.

Some visitors confidently assert that these texts are religious works, calling them mandalas or scriptures. Others confidently assert that the Nna Mmoy have no religion.

There are many traces on the Nna Mmoy plane of what people from our plane call civilisation, by which people from our plane, these days, usually mean a capitalist economy and an industrial technology based on intense, exhaustive exploitation of natural and human resources.

Ruins of immense cities, traces of long roads and huge paved areas, vast wastelands of desertification and permanent pollution, and other evidences of progressive society and advanced scientific technology crop up among the fields and border the parklands. All are very ancient and seem to be quite meaningless to the Nna Mmoy, who regard them without awe or interest.

Which is how they also regard visitors.

No one understands the language well enough to know if the Nna Mmoy have any history or legends of the ancestors responsible for the vast works and destructions that litter their placid landscape.

My friend Laure says that he heard the Nna Mmoy use a word in connection with the ruins: *nen*. As well as he could figure out, the syllable *nen,* variously modified by the syllables that surround it, may signify a range of objects from a flash flood to a tiny iridescent beetle. He thought the central area of connotation of *nen* might be "things that move fast" or "events occurring quickly." It seems an odd name to give the timeless, grass-grown ruins that loom above the villages or serve as their foundations—the cracked and sunken tracts of pavement that are now the silted bottoms of shallow lakes—the immense chemical deserts where nothing grows except a thin, purplish bloom of bacteria on poisonous water seeps.

But then, it's not certain that anything has a name in Nna Mmoy.

Laure has spent more time in the "garden utopia" than most people. I asked him to write me anything he wanted about it. He sent the following letter:

You asked about the language. You've described the problem well, I think. It might help to think of it this way:

We talk snake. A snake can go any direction but only one direction at one time, following its head.

They talk starfish. A starfish doesn't go anywhere much. It has no head. It keeps more choices handy, even if it doesn't use them.

I imagine that starfish don't think about alternatives, like left or right, forward or back; they'd think in terms of five kinds of lefts and rights, five kinds of backs and forths. Or twenty kinds of lefts and rights, twenty kinds of backs and forths. The only either/or for a starfish would be up and down. The other dimensions or directions or choices would be either/or/or/or/or...

Well, that describes one aspect of their language. When you say something in Nna Mmoy, there is a center to what you say, but the statement goes in more than one direction from the center—or to the center.

In Japanese, I'm told, a slight modification in one word or reference changes a sentence entirely, so that—I don't know Japanese, I'm making this up—if a syllable changes in one word, then "the crickets are singing in chorus in the starlight" becomes "the taxicabs are in gridlock at the intersection." I gather that Japanese poetry uses these almost-double meanings deliberately. A line of poetry can be translucent, as it were, to another meaning it could have if it were in a different context. The surface significance allows a possible alternate significance to register at the same time.

Well, everything you say in Nna Mmoy is like that. Every statement is transparent to other possible statements because the meaning of every word is contingent on the meanings of the words around it. Which is why you probably can't call them words.

A word in our languages is a real thing, a sound with a fixed form to it. Take *cat*. In a sentence or standing by itself, it has a meaning: a certain kind of animal; in talking it's the same three phonemes, and in writing the same three letters *c, a, t,* plus maybe *s,* and there it is, *cat*. As distinct as a pebble. Or as a cat. Cat is a noun. Verbs are a little shiftier. What does it mean if you say the word *had*? All by itself? Not much. *Had* isn't like *cat,* it needs context, a subject, an object.

No word in Nna Mmoy is like *cat*. Every word in Nna Mmoy is like *had,* only more so, much more so.

Take the syllable *dde*. It doesn't have a meaning yet. *A no dde mü as,* that means more or less "Let's go into the woods"; in that context *dde* is "woods." But if you say *Dim a dde mü as,* that means, more or less, "The tree stands beside the road": *dde* is "tree" and *a* is "road" instead of "go," and *as* is "beside" instead of "into." But then if that connotation group occurred inside other groups, it would change again—*Hse vuy u no a dde mü as med as hro se se:* "The travelers came through the desert where nothing grows." Now *dde* is "desert land," not "trees." And in *o be k'a dde k'a,* the syllable *dde* means "generous, giving freely"—nothing to do with trees at all, unless maybe metaphorically. The phrase means, more or less, "Thank you."

The range of meanings of a syllable isn't infinite, of course, but I don't think you could make a list of the possible or potential meanings. Not even a long list, like the entry for a syllable in Chinese dictionaries. A spoken Chinese syllable, *hsing* or *lung,* may have dozens of meanings; but it's still a word, even though its meaning depends to some extent on context, and even if it takes fifty different written characters to express the different meanings. Each different meaning of the syllable is in fact a different word, an entity, a pebble in the great riverbed of the language.

A Nna Mmoy syllable only has one written character. But it's not a pebble. It's a drop in the river.

Learning Nna Mmoy is like learning to weave water.

I believe it's just as difficult for them to learn their language as it is for us. But then, they have enough time, so it doesn't matter. Their lives don't start here and run to there, like ours, like horses on a racecourse. They live in the middle of time, like a starfish in its own center. Like the sun in its light.

What little I know of the language—and I'm not really certain of any of it, despite my learned disquisition on *dde*—I learned mostly from children. Their children's words are more like our words, you can expect them to mean the same thing in different sentences. But the children keep learning; and when they begin learning to read and write, at ten or so, they begin to talk more like the adults; and by the time they're adolescents I couldn't understand much of what they said—unless they talked baby talk to me. Which they often did. Learning to read and write is a lifelong occupation. I suspect it involves not only learning the characters but inventing new ones, and new combinations of them—beautiful new patterns of meaning.

They're gardeners. Things there pretty much grow on their own—no weeding, no weeds, no spraying, no pests. Still, you know how it is, in a garden there's always something to be done. In the village where I stayed there was always somebody working away in the gardens and among the trees. Nobody ever wore themselves out doing it. Then they'd gather, along in the afternoon, under the trees, and they'd talk and laugh, having one of their long, long conversations.

The talking often ended up with people reciting, or getting out a paper or a book and reading from it. Some of them would already be off reading by themselves, or writing. A lot of people wrote every day, very slowly, of course, on flimsy bits of the paper they make out of cotton plant. They might bring that piece of writing to the group in the afternoon and pass it around, and people would read from it aloud. Or some people would be at the village workshop working on a piece of jewelry, the circlets and brooches and complicated necklaces they make out of gold wire and opals and amethysts and such. When those were finished they'd get shown around too, and given away, and worn first by one person then another; nobody kept those pieces. They passed around. There was some of the shell money in the village, and sometimes, if somebody won a heap of it playing ten-tiles, they'd offer the owner of a fine piece of jewelry a shell or two for it, usually with a good deal of laughter and what seemed to be ritual insults. Some of the pieces of jewelry were wonderful things, delicate armpieces like endless filigree, or great massive necklaces shaped like starbursts and interlocking spirals. Several times I was given one. That's when I learned to say *o be k'a dde k'a.* I'd wear it for a while, and pass it on. Much as I would have liked to keep it.

I finally realised that some of the pieces of jewelry were sentences, or lines of poems. Maybe they all were.

There was a village school under a nut tree. The climate is very mild and dull, it never varies, so you can live outdoors. It seemed to be all right with everybody if I sat in at school and lis-

tened. Children would gather under that tree daily and play, until one or another of the villagers showed up and taught them
one thing or another. Most of it seemed to be language practice,
by way of storytelling. The teacher would start a story and then
a child would carry it on a way, and then another would pick it
up, and so on, everybody listening very intently, alert, ready to
take over. The subjects were just village doings, as far as I could
tell, pretty dull stuff, but there were twists and jokes, and an
unexpected or inventive usage or connection caused a lot of
pleasure and praise—"A jewel!" they'd all say. Now and then a
regular teacher would wander by, doing a round of the villages,
and have a session for a day or two or three, teaching writing
and reading. Adolescents and some adults would come to hear
the teacher, along with the children. That's how I learned to read
a few characters in certain texts.

The villagers never tried to ask me about myself or where I
came from. They had no curiosity of that kind at all. They were
kind, patient, generous, sharing food, giving me a house, letting
me work with them, but they were not interested in me. Or in
anything, as far as I could tell, except their daily pursuits—gardening, preparing food, making jewelry, writing, and conversation. But conversation only with one another.

Like everybody else, I found their language so difficult that
they probably thought me retarded. I made the usual attempts to
learn by exchanging words—you hit your chest and say your
name and look inquiringly at the person facing you—you hold
up a leaf and say "leaf" and look hopefully at the person facing
you...They simply did not respond. Not even the young
children.

As far as I can tell, a Nna Mmoy does not have a name. They address one another by ever-varying phrases which seem to signify both permanent and temporary relationships of consanguinity, of responsibility and dependence, of contingent status, of a thousand social and emotional connections. I could point to myself and say "Laure," but what relationship would that signify?

I suspect they heard my language as a noise made by an idiot.

Nothing else in their world speaks. Nothing else has sentience, let alone intelligence. In their world there is only one language. They recognised me as a human being, but as a defective one. I couldn't talk. I couldn't make the connections.

I had with me a magazine, a publication of an American conservation organisation, which I'd been reading in the airport. I brought it out one day and offered it to the conversation group. They didn't ask about the text or look at it with any interest. I'm sure they didn't recognise it as writing—a couple of dozen black characters, repeated endlessly in straight lines—nothing remotely like their marvelous swirls and fern fronds and interlocking superimplicated patterns. But they did look at the pictures. The magazine was full of color photographs of animals, endangered species—coral reefs and their fish, Florida panthers, manatees, California condors. It passed around the village, and people from other villages asked to look at it when they came visiting and bartering and conversing.

They showed it to the schoolteacher when she came on her rounds, and she asked me about the pictures, the only time any Nna Mmoy tried to ask me a question. I think what she was asking was *Who are these people?*

In their world, you know, there are no animals but themselves. Except for little, harmless bees and flies, that pollinate plants or break down dead matter. All the plants are edible. The grass is a nourishing grain. Five kinds of trees, that all bear fruit or nuts. One kind of evergreen, used for wood, and it has edible nuts too. One ubiquitous shrub, a cotton bush which produces fiber to spin, edible roots, and leaves for tea. Aside from the necessary bacteria there aren't more than twenty or thirty species of animal or plant in the world. All of them, including the bacteria, are "useful" and "harmless"—to human beings.

Life there is a product of engineering. It was designed. Utopia indeed. Everything human beings need and nothing they don't need. Panthers, condors, manatees—who needs them?

Rornan's *Planary Guide* says the Nna Mmoy are "degenerate remnants of a great ancient culture." Rornan has things backward. What is degenerate on their plane is the web of life. The "great ancient culture" took a vast, rich, incalculably complex tapestry, like the life that clothes our world, and reduced it to a miserable scrap.

I am certain this terrible poverty dates from the age of the ruins. Their ancestors, with all the resources of science and all the best intentions, robbed them blind. Our world is full of diseases, enemies, waste, and danger, those ancestors said—hostile microbes and viruses infecting us, noxious weeds growing thick about us while we starve, useless animals that carry plagues and poisons and compete with us for air and food and water. This world is too hard for human beings to live in, too hard for our children, they said, but we know how to make it easy.

So they did. They eliminated everything that was not useful.

They took a great complex pattern and simplified it to perfection. A nursery room safe for the children. A theme park where people have nothing to do but enjoy themselves.

But the Nna Mmoy outwitted their ancestors, at least in part. They've made the pattern back into something endlessly complicated, infinitely rich, and without any rational use. They do it with words.

They don't have any representative arts. They decorate their pottery and whatever else they make only with their beautiful writing. The only way they imitate the world is by putting words together: that is, by letting words interrelate in a fertile, ever-changing complexity to form shapes and patterns that have never existed before, beautiful forms that exist briefly and create and give way to other forms. Their language is their own exuberant, endlessly proliferating ecology. All the jungle they have, all the wilderness, is their poetry.

As I said, the pictures in my magazine interested them, the pictures of animals. They gazed at them with what seemed to me an uncomprehending wistfulness. I told them the names, pointing out the word written as I spoke it. And they'd repeat: *Pan dhedh. Kon dodh. Ma na tii.*

Those were the only words of my language they ever listened to, recognising that they had meaning.

I suppose they understood as much from those words as I did from the syllables of their language that I learned: very little, and probably all wrong.

I wandered around the ancient ruins near the village sometimes. I found a wall that had been revealed when one of the villages used the place as a rock quarry. There was a carving, a bas-relief, worn away by the ages, but as I studied it I began to see what it was: a procession of people, and there were other creatures in the procession. It was hard to make out what they were. Animals, certainly. Some were four-legged. One had great horns or wings. They might have been real animals or imaginary, or figures of animal gods. I tried to ask the teacher about them, but she just said, "*Nen, nen.*"

The Building

≈

From the unpublished Voyages to Qoq, Rehik, and Djg, *by Thomas Atall, with the kind permission of the author*

The plane of Qoq is unusual in having two rational, or more or less rational, species.

The Daqo are stocky, greenish-tan-colored humanoids. The Aq are taller and a little greener than the Daqo. The two species, though diverged from a common simioid ancestor, cannot interbreed.

Something over four thousand years ago the Daqo had what the *Planar Encyclopedia* refers to as an EEPT: a period of explosive expansion of population and technology.

Before it, the two species had seldom come in contact. The Aq inhabited the southern continent, the Daqo were in the northern hemisphere. The Daqo population escalated, spreading out over the three landmasses of the northern hemisphere and then to the south. As they conquered their world, they incidentally conquered the Aq.

The Daqo attempted to use the Aq as slaves for domestic or factory work but failed. It seems the Aq, though unaggressive, do not take orders. During the height of the EEPT the most expansive Daqo nations pursued a policy of slaughtering the "primitive" and "unteachable" Aq in the name of progress. Settlers of the equatorial zone pushed the remnant Aq populations farther south yet, into the deserts and the barely habitable canebrakes of the coast.

All species on Qoq, except a few pests and the insuperable and indifferent bacteria, suffered badly during and after the Daqo EEPT. In the final ecocatastrophe, the Daqo population dropped by four billion in four decades. The species has survived, living on a modest scale, vastly reduced in numbers and more interested in survival than dominion.

As for the Aq, probably very few, perhaps only hundreds, survived the rapid destruction and final ruin of the planet's life web.

Descent from this limited genetic source may help explain the prevalence of certain traits among the Aq, but the cultural expression of these tendencies is inexplicable in its uniformity. We don't know much about what they were like before the crash, but their reputed refusal to carry out the other species' orders suggests that they were already working, as it were, under orders of their own.

There are now about two million Daqo, mostly on the coasts of the south and the northwest continents. They live in small cities, towns, and farms and carry on agriculture and commerce; their technology is efficient but modest, limited both by the exhaustion of their world's resources and by strict religious sanctions.

There are probably fifteen or twenty thousand Aq, all on the southern continent. They live as gatherers and fishers, with some limited, casual agriculture. The only one of their domesticated animals to survive the die-offs is the boos, a clever creature descended from pack-hunting carnivores. The Aq hunted with boos when there were animals to hunt. Since the crash, they use boos to carry or haul light loads, as companions, and in hard times as food.

Aq villages are movable; from time immemorial their houses have been fabric domes stretched on a frame of light poles or canes, easy to set up, dismantle, and transport. The tall cane which grows in the swampy lakes of the desert and all along the coasts of the equatorial zone of the southern continent is their staple; they gather the young shoots for food, spin and weave the fiber into cloth, and make rope, baskets, and tools from the stems. When they have used up all the cane in a region, they pick up the village and move on. The cane plants regenerate from the root system in a few years.

The Aq have kept pretty much to the desert-and-canebrake habitat enforced upon them by the Daqo in earlier millennia. Some, however, camp around outside Daqo towns and engage in a little barter and filching. The Daqo trade with them for their fine canvas and baskets, and tolerate their thievery to a surprising degree.

Indeed the Daqo attitude to the Aq is hard to define. Wariness is part of it; a kind of unease that is not suspicion or distrust; a watchfulness that, surprisingly, stops short of animosity or contempt, and may even become conciliating.

It is even harder to say what the Aq think of the Daqo. The two populations communicate in a pidgin or jargon containing elements from both languages, but it appears that no individual ever learns the other species' language. The two species seem to have settled on coexistence without relationship. They have nothing to do with each other except for these occasional, slightly abrasive contacts at the edges of southern Daqo settlements—and a limited, very strange collaboration having to do with what I can only call the specific obsession of the Aq.

I am not comfortable with the phrase "specific obsession," but "cultural instinct" is worse.

At about two and a half or three years old, Aq babies begin building. Whatever comes into their little greeny-bronze hands that can possibly serve as a block or brick they pile up into "houses." The Aq use the same word for these miniature structures as for the fragile cane-and-canvas domes they live in, but there is no resemblance except that both are roofed enclosures with a door. The children's "houses" are rectangular, flat-roofed, and always made of solid, heavy materials. They are not imitations of Daqo houses, or only at a very great remove, since most of these children have never been to a Daqo town, never seen a Daqo building.

It is hard to believe that they imitate one another with such unanimity that they never vary the plan; but it is even harder to believe that their building style, like that of insects, is innate.

As the children get older and more skillful they build larger constructions, though still no more than knee high, with passages, courtyards, and sometimes towers. Many children spend all their free time gathering rocks or making mud bricks and building "houses." They do not populate their buildings with toy people or animals or tell stories about them. They just build them, with evident pleasure and satisfaction. By the age of six or seven some children begin to leave off building, but others go on working together with other children, often under the guidance of interested adults, to make "houses" of considerable complexity, though still not large enough for anyone to live in. The children do not play in them.

When the village picks up and moves to a new gathering ground or canebrake, these children leave their constructions behind without any sign of distress. As soon as they are settled, they begin building again, often cannibalising stones or bricks from the "houses" a previous generation left on the site. Popular gathering sites are marked by dozens or hundreds of solidly built miniature ruins, populated only by the joint-legged gikoto of the marshes or the little ratlike hikiqi of the desert.

No such ruins have been found in areas where the Aq lived before the Daqo conquest. Evidently their propensity to build was less strong, or didn't exist, before the conquest, or before the crash.

Two or three years after their ceremonies of adolescence some of the young people, those who went on building "houses" until they reached puberty, will go on their first stone faring.

A stone faring sets out once a year from the Aq territories. The complete journey takes from two to three years, after which the travelers return to their natal village for five or six years. Some Aq never go stone faring, others go once, some go several or many times in their life.

The route of the stone farings is to the coast of Riqim, on the northeast continent, and back to the Mediro, a rocky plateau far inland from the southernmost canebrakes of the great south continent.

The Aq stone farers gather in spring, coming overland or by cane raft from their various villages to Gatbam, a small port near the equator on the west coast. There a fleet of cane-and-canvas sailboats awaits them. The sailors and navigators are all Daqo of the south continent. They are professional sailors, mostly fishermen; some of them "sail the faring" every year for decades. The Aq pilgrims have nothing to pay them with, arriving with provisions for the journey but nothing else. While at Riqim, the Daqo sailors will net and salt fish from those rich waters, a catch which makes their journey profitable. But they never go to fish off Riqim except with the stone-faring fleet.

The journey takes several weeks. The voyage north is the dangerous one, made early in the year so that the return voyage, carrying the cargo, may be made at the optimal time. Now and then boats or even whole fleets are lost in the wild tropical storms of that wide sea.

As soon as they disembark on the stony shores of Riqim, the Aq get to work. Under the direction of senior stone farers, the novices set up domed tents, store their sparse provisions, take up the tools left there by the last pilgrimage, and climb the steep green cliffs to the quarries.

Riqimite is a lustrous, fine-textured, greenish stone with a tendency to cleave along a plane. It can be sawed in blocks or split into stone planks or smaller tiles and even into sheets so thin they are translucent. Though relatively light, it is stone, and a ten-meter canvas sailboat can't carry great quantities of it; so the stone farers carefully gauge the amount they quarry. They rough-shape the blocks at Riqim and even do some of the fine cutting, so that the boats carry as little waste as possible. They work fast, since they want to start home in the calm season around the solstice. When their work is complete they run up a flag on a high pole on the cliffs to signal the Daqo fleet, which comes in boat by boat over the next few days. They load the stone aboard under the tubs of salted fish and set sail back south.

The boats put in at one Daqo port or another, usually the crew's home port, to unload and sell their fish; then they all sail on several hundred kilometers down the coast to Gazt, a long, shallow harbor in the hot marshlands south of the canebrake country. There the sailors help the Aq unload the stone. They receive no payment for or profit from this part of the trip.

I asked a shipmaster who had "sailed the faring" many times why she and her sailors were willing to take the Aq stone farers down to Gazt. She shrugged. "It's part of the agreement," she said, evidently not having thought much about it. After thinking, she added, "Be an awful job to drag that stone overland through the marshes."

Before the Daqo boats have sailed halfway back to the harbor mouth, the Aq have begun loading the stone onto wheeled flatbed carts left on the docks of Gazt by the last stone faring.

Then they get into harness and haul these carts five hundred kilometers inland and three thousand meters upward.

They go at most three or four kilometers a day. They encamp before evening and fan out from the trails to forage and set snares for hikiqi, since by now their supplies are low. The cart train follows the least recently used of the several winding trails, because the hunting and gathering will be better along it.

During the sea voyages and at Riqim the mood of the stone farers tends to be solemn and tense. They are not sailors, and the labor at the quarries is hard and driven. Hauling carts by shoulder harness is certainly not light work either, but the pilgrims take it merrily; they talk and joke while hauling, share their food and sit talking around their campfires, and behave like any group of people engaged willingly in an arduous joint enterprise.

They discuss which path to take, and wheel-mending techniques, and so on. But when I went with them I never heard them talk in the larger sense about what they were doing, their journey's goal.

All the paths finally have to surmount the cliffs at the edge of the plateau. As the stone farers come up onto the level after that terrible last grade, they stop and gaze to the southeast. One after another the long, flat carts laden with dusty stone buck and jerk up over the rim and stop. The haulers stand in harness, gazing silent at the Building.

After hundreds of years of the slow recovery of the shattered ecosystem, enough Aq began to have enough food to have enough energy for activities beyond forage and storage. It was then, when bare survival was still chancy, that they began the stone faring.

So few of them, in such an inimical world, the atmosphere damaged, the great cycles of life not yet reestablished in the poisoned and despoiled oceans, the lands full of bones, ghosts, ruins, dead forests, deserts of salt, of sand, of chemical waste—how did the inhabitants of such a world think of undertaking such a task? How did they know the stone they wanted was at Riqim? How did they know where Riqim was? Did they originally make their way there somehow without Daqo boats and navigators? The origins of the stone faring are absolutely mysterious, but no more mysterious than its object. All we know is that every stone in the Building comes from the quarries of Riqim, and that the Aq have been building it for over three thousand, perhaps four thousand years.

It is immense, of course. It covers many acres and contains thousands of rooms, passages, and courts. It is certainly one of the largest edifices, perhaps the largest single one, on any world we know. And yet declarations of size, counts and measures, comparisons and superlatives, are meaningless. The fact is, a technology such as that of contemporary Earth, or the ancient Daqo, could build a building ten times bigger in ten years.

It is possible that the ever-increasing vastness of the Building is a metaphor or illustration of precisely such a factual enormity.

Or the Building's size may be purely a result of its age. The oldest sections, far inside its outermost walls, show no indication that they were—or were not—seen as the beginning of something immense. They are exactly like the Aq children's "houses" on a larger scale.

All the rest of the Building has been added on, year by year, to this modest beginning, in much the same style. After perhaps some centuries the builders began to add stories onto the flat roofs of the early Building, but have never gone above four stories, except for towers and pinnacles and the airy barrel domes that reach a height of perhaps sixty meters. The great bulk of the Building is no more than five to six meters high. Inevitably it has kept growing outwards laterally, by way of ells and wings and joining arcades and courtyards, until it covers so vast an area that from a distance it looks like a fantastic terrain, a low mountain landscape all in silvery green stone.

Although not dwarfish like the children's structures, curiously enough the Building is not quite full scale, taking the average height of an Aq as measure. The ceilings are barely high enough to allow them to stand straight, and they must stoop to pass through the doors.

No part of the Building is ruined or in disrepair, though occasional earthquakes shake the Mediro plateau. Damaged areas are repaired annually, or "mined" for stone to rebuild with.

The work is fine, careful, sure, and delicate. No material is used but riqimite, mortised and tenoned like wood, or set in exquisitely fitted blocks and courses. The indoor surfaces are mostly finished satin smooth, the outer faces left in contrasting degrees of roughness and smoothness. There is no carving or ornamentation other than thin moldings or incised lines repeating and outlining the architectural shapes.

Windows are unglazed stone lattices or pierced stone sheets cut so thin as to be translucent. The repetitive rectangular designs of the latticework are elegantly proportioned; a ratio of three to two runs through many though not all of the Building's rooms and apertures. Doors are thin stone slabs so well balanced and pivoted that they swing lightly and smoothly open and shut. There are no furnishings.

Empty rooms, empty corridors, miles of corridors, endlessly similar stairways, ramps, courtyards, roof terraces, delicate towers, vistas of roof beyond roof, tower beyond tower, dome beyond dome to the far distance; high rooms lighted by great lacework windows or only by the dim, greenish, mottled translucency of windowpanes of stone; corridors that lead to other corridors, other rooms, stairs, ramps, courtyards, corridors...Is it a maze, a labyrinth? Yes, inevitably; but is that what it was built to be?

Is it beautiful? Yes, in a way, wonderfully beautiful; but is that what it was built to be?

The Aq are a rational species. They have language. Answers to these questions must come from them.

The troubling thing is that they have many different answers, none of which seems quite satisfying to them or anyone else.

In this they resemble any reasonable being who does an unreasonable thing and justifies it with reasons. War, for example. My species has a great many good reasons for making war, though none of them is as good as the reason for not making war. Our most rational and scientific justifications—for instance, that we are an aggressive species—are perfectly circular: we make war because we make war. Our justifications for making a particular war (such as: our people must have more land and more wealth, or: our people must have more power, or: our people must obey our deity's orders to crush the sacrilegious infidel) all come down to the same thing: we must make war because we must. We have no choice. We have no freedom. This argument is not ultimately satisfactory to the reasoning mind, which desires freedom.

In the same way, the efforts of the Aq to explain or justify their building and their Building all invoke a necessity which doesn't seem all that necessary and use reasons which meet themselves coming around. We go stone faring because we have always done it. We go to Riqim because the best stone is there. The Building is on the Mediro because the ground's good and there's room for it there. The Building is a great undertaking, which our children can look forward to and our men and women can work together on. The stone faring brings people from all our villages together. We were only a poor scattered people in the old days, but now the Building shows that there is a great vision in us. —All these reasons make sense but don't convince, don't satisfy.

Perhaps the questions should be asked of those Aq who never have gone stone faring. They don't question the stone faring. They speak of the stone farers as people doing something brave, difficult, worthy, perhaps sacred. So why have you never gone yourself? —Well, I never felt the need to. People who go, they have to go, they're called to it.

What about the other people, the Daqo? What do they think about this immense structure, certainly the greatest enterprise and achievement on their world at this time? Very little, evidently. Even the sailors of the stone faring never go up onto the Mediro and know nothing about the Building except that it is there and is very large. Daqo of the northwest continent know it only as rumor, fable, travelers' tales of the "Palace of the Mediro" on the Great South Continent. Some tales say the King of the Aq lives there in unimaginable splendor; some say that it is a tower taller than the mountains, in which eyeless monsters dwell; others that it is a maze where the unwary traveler is lost in endless corridors full of bones and ghosts; others that the winds blowing through it moan in huge chords like a vast aeolian harp, which can be heard for hundreds of miles; and so on. To the Daqo it is a legend, like their own legends of the ancient times when their mighty ancestors flew in the air and drank rivers dry and turned forests into stone and built towers taller than the sky, and so on. Fairy tales.

Now and then an Aq who has been stone faring will say something different about the Building. If asked about it, some of them reply: "It is for the Daqo."

Indeed the Building is better proportioned to the short stature of the Daqo than to the tall Aq. The Daqo, if they ever went there, could walk through the corridors and doorways upright.

An old woman of Katas, who had been five times a stone farer, was the first who gave me that answer.

"The Building is for the Daqo?" I said, taken aback. "But why?"

"Because of the old days."

"But they never go there."

"It isn't finished," she said.

"A retribution?" I asked, puzzling at it. "A recompense?"

"They need it," she said.

"The Daqo need it, but you don't?"

"No," the old woman said with a smile. "We build it. We don't need it."

The Fliers of Gy

≋

The people of Gy look pretty much like people from our plane except that they have plumage, not hair. A fine, fuzzy down on the heads of infants becomes a soft, short coat of speckled dun on the fledglings, and with adolescence this grows out into a full head of feathers. Most men have ruffs at the back of the neck, shorter feathers all over the head, and tall, erectile crests. The head plumage of males is brown or black, barred and marked variously with bronze, red, green, and blue. Women's plumes usually grow long, sometimes sweeping down the back almost to the floor, with soft, curling, trailing edges, like the tails of ostriches; the colors of the feathers of women are vivid—purple, scarlet, coral, turquoise, gold. Gyr men and women are downy in the pubic region and pit of the arm and often have short, fine plumage over the whole body. People with brightly colored body feathers are a cheerful sight when naked, but they are much troubled by lice and nits.

Moulting is a continuous process, not seasonal. As people age, not all the moulted feathers grow back, and patchy baldness is common among both men and women over forty. Most people, therefore, save the best of their head feathers as they moult out, to make into wigs or false crests as needed. Those whose plumage is scanty or dull can also buy feather wigs at special shops. There are fads for bleaching one's feathers or spraying them gold or curling them, and wig shops in the cities will bleach, dye, spray, or crimp one's plumage and sell headdresses in whatever the current fashion is. Poor women with specially long, splendid head feathers often sell them to the wig shops for a fairly good price.

The Gyr write with quill pens. It is traditional for a father to give a set of his own stiff ruff quills to a child beginning to learn to write. Lovers exchange feathers with which they write love letters to one another, a pretty custom, referred to in a famous scene in the play *The Misunderstanding* by Inuinui:

> *O my betraying plume, that wrote his love*
> *To her! His love—my feather, and my blood!*

The Gyr are a staid, steady, traditional people, uninterested in innovation, shy of strangers. They are resistant to technological invention and novelty; attempts to sell them ballpoint pens or airplanes, or to induce them to enter the wonderful world of electronics, have failed. They continue writing letters to one another with quill pens, calculating with their heads, walking afoot or riding in carriages pulled by large, doglike animals called ugnunu, learning a few words in foreign languages when absolutely necessary, and watching classic stage plays written in traditional meters. No amount of exposure to the useful technologies, the marvelous gadgets, the advanced scientific knowledge of other planes—for Gy is a fairly popular tourist stop—seems to rouse envy or greed or a sense of inferiority in the Gyran bosom. They go on doing exactly as they have always done, not stodgily, exactly, but with a kind of dullness, a polite indifference and impenetrability, behind which may lie supreme self-satisfaction, or something quite different.

The crasser kind of tourists from other planes refer to the Gyr, of course, as birdies, birdbrains, featherheads, and so on. Many visitors from livelier planes visit the small, placid cities, take rides out into the country in ugnunu chaises, attend sedate but charming balls (for the Gyr like to dance), and enjoy an old-fashioned evening at the theater, without losing one degree of their contempt for the natives. "Feathers but no wings" is the conventional judgment that sums it up.

Such patronising visitors may spend a week in Gy without ever seeing a winged native or learning that what they took for a bird or a jet was a woman on her way across the sky.

The Gyr don't talk about their winged people unless asked. They don't conceal them or lie about them, but they don't volunteer information. I had to ask questions fairly persistently to be able to write the following description.

Wings never develop before late adolescence. There is no sign at all of the propensity until suddenly a girl of eighteen, a boy of nineteen, wakes up with a slight fever and an ache in the shoulder blades.

After that comes a year or more of great physical stress and pain, during which the subject must be kept quiet, warm, and well-fed. Nothing gives comfort but food—the nascent fliers are terribly hungry most of the time—and being wrapped or swaddled in blankets, while the body restructures, remakes, rebuilds itself. The bones lighten and become porous, the whole upper body musculature changes, and bony protuberances, developing rapidly from the shoulder blades, grow out into immense alar processes. The final stage is the growth of the wing feathers, which is not painful. The primaries are, as feathers go, massive, and may be a meter long. The wingspread of an adult male Gyr is about four meters, that of a woman usually about a half meter less. Stiff feathers sprout from the calves and ankles, to be spread wide in flight.

Any attempt to interfere, to prevent or halt the growth of wings, is useless and harmful or fatal. If the wings are not allowed to develop, the bones and muscles begin to twist and shrivel, causing unendurable, unceasing pain. Amputation of the wings or the flight feathers, at any stage, results in a slow, agonising death.

Among some of the most conservative, archaic peoples of the Gyr, the tribal societies living along the icy coasts of the north polar regions and the herdsfolk of the cold, barren steppes of the far south, this vulnerability of the winged people is incorporated into religion and ritual behavior. In the north, as soon as a youth shows the fatal signs, he or she is captured and handed over to the tribal elders. With rituals similar to their funeral rites, they fasten heavy stones to the victim's hands and feet, then go in procession to a cliff high above the sea and push the victim over, shouting, "Fly! Fly for us!"

Among the steppe tribes, the wings are allowed to develop completely, and the youth is carefully, worshipfully attended all that year. Let us say that it is a girl who has shown the fatal symptoms. In her feverish trances she functions as a shaman and soothsayer. The priests listen and interpret all her sayings to the people. When her wings are full grown, they are bound down to her back. Then the whole tribe set out to walk with her to the nearest high place, cliff or crag—often a journey of weeks in that flat, desolate country.

On the heights, after days of dancing and imbibing hallucinatory smoke from smudge fires of byubyu wood, the priests go with the young woman, all of them drugged, dancing and singing, to the edge of the cliff. There her wings are freed. She lifts them for the first time, and then like a young falcon leaving the nest, leaps stumbling off the cliff into the air, wildly beating those huge, untried wings. Whether she flies or falls, all the men of the tribe, screaming with excitement, shoot at her with bow and arrow or throw their razor-pointed hunting spears. She falls, pierced by dozens of spears and arrows. The woman scrambles down the cliff, and if there is any life left in her, they beat it out with stones. They then throw and heap stones over the body till it is buried under a cairn.

There are many cairns at the foot of every steep hill or crag in all the steppe country. Ancient cairns furnish stones for the new ones.

Such young people may try to escape their fate by running

away from their people, but the weakness and fever that attend the development of wings cripple them, and they never get far.

There is a folktale in the South Marches of Merm of a winged man who leapt up into the air from the sacrificial crag and flew so strongly that he escaped the spears and arrows and disappeared into the sky. The original story ends there. The playwright Norwer used it as the basis of a romantic tragedy. In his play *Transgression,* the young man has appointed a tryst with his beloved and flies there to meet with her; but she has unwittingly betrayed him to another suitor, who lies in wait. As the lovers embrace, the suitor hurls his spear and kills the winged one. The maiden pulls out her own knife and kills the murderer and then—after exchanging anguished farewells with the not quite expired winged one—stabs herself. It is melodramatic but, if well staged, very moving; everybody has tears in their eyes when the hero first descends like an eagle, and when, dying, he enfolds his beloved in his great bronze wings.

A version of *Transgression* was performed a few years ago on my plane, in Chicago, at the Actual Reality Theater. It was probably inevitably, but unfortunately, translated as *Sacrifice of the Angels.* There is absolutely no mythology or lore concerning anything like our angels among the Gyr. Sentimental pictures of sweet little cherubs with baby wings, hovering guardian spirits, or grander images of divine messengers would strike them as a hideous mockery of something every parent and every adolescent dreads: a rare but fearful deformity, a curse, a death sentence.

Among the urbanised Gyr, that dread is mitigated to some degree, since the winged ones are treated not as sacrificial scape-

goats but with tolerance and even sympathy, as people with a most unfortunate handicap.

We may find this odd. To soar over the heads of the earth-bound, to race with eagles and soar with condors, to dance on air, to ride the wind, not in a noisy metal box or on a contraption of plastic and fabric and straps but on one's own vast, strong, splendid, outstretched wings—how could that be anything but a joy, a freedom? How stodgy, sullen-hearted, leaden-souled the Gyr must be, to think that people who can fly are cripples!

But they do have their reasons. The fact is that the winged Gyr can't trust their wings.

No fault can be found in the actual design of the wings. They serve admirably, with a little practice, for short flights, for effortless gliding and soaring on updrafts and, with more practice, for stunts and tumbling, aerial acrobatics. When winged people are fully mature, if they fly regularly they may achieve great stamina. They can stay aloft almost indefinitely. Many learn to sleep on the wing. Flights of over two thousand miles have been recorded, with only brief hover-stops to eat. Most of these very long flights were made by women, whose lighter bodies and bone structure give them the advantage over distance. Men, with their more powerful musculature, would take the speed-flying awards, if there were any. But the Gyr, at least the wingless majority, are not interested in records or awards, certainly not in competitions that involve a high risk of death.

The problem is that fliers' wings are liable to sudden, total, disastrous failure. Flight engineers and medical investigators on Gyr and elsewhere have not been able to account for it. The design of the wings has no detectable fault; their failure must be caused by an as yet unidentified physical or psychological factor, an incompatibility of the alar processes with the rest of the body. Unfortunately no weakness shows up beforehand; there is no way to predict wing failure. It occurs without warning. A flier who has flown his entire adult life without a shadow of trouble takes off one morning and, having attained altitude, suddenly, appallingly, finds his wings will not obey him—they are shuddering, closing, clapping down along his sides, paralysed. And he falls from the sky like a stone.

The medical literature states that as many as one flight in twenty ends in failure. Fliers I talked to believe that wing failure is not nearly as frequent as that, citing cases of people who have flown daily for decades. But it is not a matter they want to talk about with me, or perhaps even with one another. They seem to have no preventive precautions or rituals, accepting it as truly random. Failure may come on the first flight or the thousandth. No cause has been found for it—heredity, age, inexperience, fatigue, diet, emotion, physical condition. Every time a flier goes up, the chance of wing failure is the same.

Some survive the fall. But they never fall again, because they can never fly again. Once the wings have failed, they are useless. They remain paralysed, dragging along beside and behind their owner like a huge, heavy feather cape.

Foreigners ask why fliers don't carry parachutes in case of wing failure. No doubt they could. It is a question of temperament. Winged people who fly are those willing to take the risk of wing failure. Those who do not want the risk, do not fly. Or perhaps those who consider it a risk do not fly, and those who fly do not consider it a risk.

As amputation of the wings is invariably fatal, and surgical removal of any part of them causes acute, incurable, crippling pain, the fallen fliers and those who choose not to fly must drag their wings about all their lives, through the streets, up and down the stairs. Their changed bone structure is not well suited to ground life. They tire easily walking and suffer many fractures and muscular injuries. Few nonflying fliers live to sixty.

Those who do fly face their death every time they take off. Some of them, however, are still alive and still flying at eighty.

It is a quite wonderful sight, takeoff. Human beings aren't as awkward as I would have expected, having seen the graceless flapping of such masters of the air as pelicans and swans getting airborne. Of course it is easiest to launch from a perch or height, but if there's no such convenience handy, all they need is a run of twenty or twenty-five meters, enough for a couple of lifts and downbeats of the great extended wings, and then a step that doesn't touch the ground, and then they're up, aloft, soaring—maybe circling back overhead to smile and wave down at up-lifted faces before arrowing off above the roofs or over the hills.

They fly with the legs close together, the body arched a little backward, the leg feathers fanning out into a hawklike tail as needed. As the arms have no integral muscular connection to the wings—winged Gyr are six-limbed creatures—the hands may be kept down along the sides to reduce air resistance and increase speed. In a leisurely flight, they may do anything hands do—scratch the head, peel a fruit, sketch an aerial view of the landscape, hold a baby. Though the last I saw only once, and it troubled me.

I talked several times with a winged Gyr named Ardiadia; what follows is all in his own words, recorded, with his permission, during our conversations.

Oh, yes, when I first found out—when it started happening to me, you know—I was floored. Terrified! I couldn't believe it. I'd been so sure it wouldn't happen to me. When we were kids, you know, we used to joke about so-and-so being "flighty," or say, "He'll be taking off one of these days." But me? Me grow wings? It wasn't going to happen to me. So when I got this headache, and then my teeth ached for a while, and then my back began to hurt, I kept telling myself it was a toothache, I had an infection, an abscess... But when it really began, there was no more fooling myself. It was terrible. I really can't remember much about it. It was bad. It hurt. First like knives running back and forth between my shoulders, and claws digging up and down my spine. And then all over, my arms, my legs, my fingers, my face... And I was so weak I couldn't stand up. I got out of bed and fell down on the floor and I couldn't get up. I lay there calling my mother, "Mama! Mama, please come!" She was asleep. She worked late, waiting in a restaurant, and didn't get home till way after midnight, and so she slept hard. And I could feel the floor getting hot underneath me, I was so hot with fever, and I'd try to move my face to a cooler place on the floor...

Well, I don't know if the pain eased off or I just got used to it, but it was a bit better after a couple of months. It was hard, though. And long, and dull, and strange. Lying there. But not on my back. You can't lie on your back, ever, you know. Hard to sleep at night. When it hurt, it always hurt most at night. Always a little fevery, thinking strange thoughts, having funny ideas. And never able to think a thought through, never able quite to hold on to an idea. I felt as if I myself really couldn't think anymore. Thoughts just came into me and went through me and I watched them. And no plans for the future anymore, because what was my future now? I'd thought of being a schoolteacher. My mother had been so excited about that, she'd encouraged me to stay in school the extra year, to qualify for teachers' college... Well. I had my nineteenth birthday lying there in my little room in our three-room flat over the grocery on Lacemakers Lane. My mother brought some fancy food from the restaurant and a bottle of honey wine, and we tried to have a celebration, but I couldn't drink the wine, and she couldn't eat because she was crying. But I could eat, I was always starving hungry, and that cheered her up... Poor Mama!

Well, so, I came out of that, little by little, and the wings grew in, great ugly dangling naked things, disgusting, to start with, and even worse when they started to fledge, with the pinfeathers like great pimples. But when the primaries and secondaries came out, and I began to feel the muscles there, and to be able to shudder my wings, shake them, raise them a little—and I wasn't feverish anymore, or I'd got used to running a fever all the time, I'm not really sure which it is—and I was able to get up and walk around, and feel how light my body was now, as if gravity couldn't affect me, even with the weight of those huge wings dragging after me...but I could lift them, get them up off the floor...

Not myself, though. I was earthbound. My body felt light, but I wore out even trying to walk, got weak and shaky. I used to be pretty good at the broad jump, but now I couldn't get both feet off the ground at once.

I was feeling a lot better, but it bothered me to be so weak, and I felt closed in. Trapped. Then a flier came by, a man from uptown, who'd heard about me. Fliers look after kids going through the change. He'd looked in a couple of times to reassure my mother and make sure I was doing all right. I was grateful for that. Now he came and talked to me for a long time, and showed me the exercises I could do. And I did them, every day, all the time—hours and hours. What else did I have to do? I used to like reading, but it didn't seem to hold my attention anymore. I used to like going to the theater, but I couldn't do that, I still wasn't strong enough. And places like theaters, they don't have room for people with unbound wings. You take up too much space, you cause a fuss. I'd been good at mathematics in school, but I couldn't fix my attention on the problems anymore. They didn't seem to matter. So I had nothing to do but the exercises the flier taught me. And I did them. All the time.

The exercises helped. There really wasn't enough room even in our sitting room, I never could do a vertical stretch fully, but I did what I could. I felt better, I got stronger. I finally began to feel like my wings were mine. Were part of me. Or I was part of them.

Then one day I couldn't stand being inside anymore. Thirteen months I'd been inside, in those three little rooms, most of them just in the one room, thirteen months! Mama was out at work. I went downstairs. I walked the first ten steps down and then I lifted my wings. Even though the staircase was way too narrow, I could lift them some, and I stepped off and floated down the last six steps. Well, sort of. I hit pretty hard at the bottom, and my knees buckled, but I didn't really fall. It wasn't flying, but it wasn't quite falling.

I went outside. The air was wonderful. I felt like I hadn't had any air for a year. Actually, I felt like I'd never known what air was in my whole life. Even in that narrow little street, with the houses hanging over it, there was wind, there was the sky, not a ceiling. The sky overhead. The air. I started walking. I hadn't planned anything. I wanted to get out of the lanes and alleys, to somewhere open, a big plaza or square or park, anything open to the sky. I saw people staring at me but I didn't care. I'd stared at people with wings, when I didn't have them. Not meaning anything, just curious. Wings aren't all that common. I used to wonder a little about what it felt like to have them, you know. Just ignorance. So I didn't care if people looked at me now. I was too eager to get out from under the roofs. My legs were weak and shaky but they kept going, and sometimes, where the street wasn't crowded with people, I'd lift my wings a little, loft them, get a feel of the air under the feathers, and for a little I'd be lighter on my feet.

So I got to the Fruit Market. The market had shut down, it was evening, the booths were all shoved back, so there was a big space in the middle, cobblestones. I stood there under the Assay Office for a while doing exercises, lifts and stretches—I could do a vertical all the way for the first time, and it felt wonderful. Then I began to trot a little as I lofted, and my feet would get off the ground for a moment, and so I couldn't resist, I couldn't help it, I began to run and to loft my wings, and then beat down, and loft again, and I was up! But there was the Weights and Measures Building right in front of me, this grey stone facade right in my face, and I actually had to fend off, push myself away from it with my hands, and drop down to the pavement. But I turned around and there I had the full run ahead of me, clear across the marketplace to the Assay Office. And I ran, and I took off.

I swooped around the marketplace for a while, staying low, learning how to turn and bank, and how to use my tail feathers. It comes pretty natural, you feel what to do, the air tells you... but the people down below were looking up, and ducking when I banked too steep, or stalled... I didn't care. I flew for over an hour, till after dark, after all the people had gone. I'd got way up over the roofs by then. But I realised my wing muscles were getting tired and I'd better come down. That was hard. I mean, landing was hard because I didn't know how to land. I came down like a sack of rocks, bam! Nearly sprained my ankle, and the soles of my feet stung like fire. If anybody saw it they must have laughed. But I didn't care. It was just hard to be on the ground. I hated being down. Limping home, dragging my wings that weren't any good here, feeling weak, feeling heavy.

It took me quite a while to get home, and Mama came in just a little after me. She looked at me and said, "You've been out," and I said, "I flew, Mama," and she burst into tears.

I was sorry for her but there wasn't much I could say.

She didn't even ask me if I was going to go on flying. She knew I would. I don't understand the people who have wings and don't use them. I suppose they're interested in having a career. Maybe they were already in love with somebody on the ground. But it seems...I don't know. I can't really understand it. *Wanting* to stay down. *Choosing* not to fly. Wingless people can't help it, it's not their fault they're grounded. But if you have wings...

Of course they may be afraid of wing failure. Wing failure doesn't happen if you don't fly. How can it? How can something fail that never worked?

I suppose being safe is important to some people. They have a family or commitments or a job or something. I don't know. You'd have to talk to one of them. I'm a flier.

I asked Ardiadia how he made his living. Like many fliers, he worked part-time for the postal service. He mostly carried government correspondence and dispatches on long flights, even overseas. Evidently he was considered a gifted and reliable employee. For particularly important dispatches, he told me that two fliers were always sent, in case one suffered wing failure.

He was thirty-two. I asked him if he was married, and he told me that fliers never married; they considered it, he said, beneath them. "Affairs on the wing," he said, with a slight smile. I asked if the affairs were always with other fliers, and he said, "Oh, yes, of course," unintentionally revealing his surprise or disgust at the idea of making love to a nonflier. His manners were pleasant and civil, he was most obliging, but he could not quite hide his sense of being apart from, different from the wingless, having nothing really to do with them. How could he help but look down on us?

I pressed him a little about this feeling of superiority, and he tried to explain. "When I said it was as if I was my wings, you know?—that's it. Being able to fly makes other things seem uninteresting. What people do seems so trivial. Flying is complete. It's enough. I don't know if you can understand. It's one's whole body, one's whole self, up in the whole sky. On a clear day, in the sunlight, with everything lying down there below, far away... Or in a high wind, in a storm—out over the sea, that's where I like best to fly. Over the sea in stormy weather. When the fishing boats run for land, and you have it all to yourself, the sky full of rain and lightning, and the clouds under your wings. Once off Emer Cape I danced with the waterspouts... It takes everything to fly. Everything you are, everything you have. And so if you go down, you go down whole. And over the sea, if you go down, that's it, who's to know, who cares? I don't want to be buried in the ground." The idea made him shiver a little. I could see the shudder in his long, heavy, bronze-and-black wing feathers.

I asked if the affairs on the wing sometimes resulted in children, and he said with indifference that of course they did. I pressed him a little about it, and he said that a baby was a great bother to a flying mother, so that as soon as it was weaned it was usually left "on the ground," as he put it, to be brought up by relatives. Sometimes the winged mother got so attached to the child that she grounded herself to look after it. He told me this with some disdain.

The children of fliers are no more likely to grow wings than other children. The phenomenon has no genetic factor but is a developmental pathology shared by all Gyr, which appears in less than one out of a thousand.

I think Ardiadia would not accept the word *pathology*.

I talked also with a nonflying winged Gyr, who let me record our conversation but asked that I not use his name. He is a member of a respectable law firm in a small city in Central Gy.

He said, "I never flew, no. I was twenty when I got sick. I'd thought I was past the age, safe. It was a terrible blow. My parents had already spent a good deal of money, made sacrifices to get me into college. I was doing well in college. I liked learning. I had an intellect. To lose a year was bad enough. I wasn't going to let this business eat up my whole life. To me the wings are simply excrescences. Growths. Impediments to walking, dancing, sitting in a civilised manner on a normal chair, wearing decent clothing. I refused to let something like that get in the way of my education, my life. Fliers are stupid, their brains go all to feathers. I wasn't going to trade in my mind for a chance to flitter about over rooftops. I'm more interested in what goes on *under* the roofs. I don't care for scenery. I prefer people. And I wanted a normal life. I wanted to marry, to have children. My father was a kind man; he died when I was sixteen, and I'd always thought that if I could be as good to my children as he was to us, it would be a way of thanking him, of honoring his memory...I was fortunate enough to meet a beautiful woman who refused to let my handicap frighten her. In fact she won't let me call it that. She insists that all this"—he indicated his wings with a slight gesture of his head—"was what she first saw in me. Claims that when we first met, she thought I was quite a boring, stuffy young fellow, till I turned around."

His head feathers were black with a blue crest. His wings, though flattened, bound, and belted down, as nonfliers' wings always are to keep them out of the way and as unnoticeable as possible, were splendidly feathered in patterns of dark blue and peacock blue with black bars and edges.

"At any rate, I was determined to keep my feet on the ground, in every sense. If I'd ever had any youthful notions about flitting off for a while, which I really never did, once I was through with the fever and delirium and had made peace with the whole painful, wasteful process—if I had ever thought of flying, once I was married, once we had a child, nothing, nothing could induce me to yearn for even a taste of that life, to consider it even for a moment. The utter irresponsibility of it, the arrogance—the arrogance of it is very distasteful to me."

We then talked for some time about his law practice, which was an admirable one, devoted to representing poor people against swindlers and profiteers. He showed me a charming portrait of his two children, eleven and nine years old, which he had drawn with one of his own quills. The chances that either child would grow wings was, as for every Gyr, a thousand to one.

Shortly before I left, I asked him, "Do you ever dream of flying?"

Lawyerlike, he was slow to answer. He looked away, out the window. "Doesn't everyone?" he said.

The Island of the Immortals

Somebody *asked me* if I'd heard that there were immortal people on the Yendian plane, and somebody else told me that
there were, so when I got there, I asked about them. The travel
agent rather reluctantly showed me on her map a place called the
Island of the Immortals. "You don't want to go there," she said.

"I don't?"

"Well, it's dangerous," she said, looking at me as if she
thought I was not the danger-loving type, in which she was entirely correct. She was a rather unpolished local agent, not an
employee of the Interplanary Service. Yendi is not a popular destination. In many ways it's so like our own plane that it seems
hardly worth the trouble of visiting. There are differences, but
they're subtle.

"Why is it called the Island of the Immortals?"

"Because some of the people there are immortal."

"They don't die?" I asked, never quite sure of the accuracy of my translatomat.

"They don't die," she said indifferently. "Now, the Prinjo Archipelago is a lovely place for a restful fortnight." Her pencil moved southward across the map of the Great Sea of Yendi. My gaze remained on the large, lonely Island of the Immortals. I pointed to it.

"Is there a hotel—there?"

"There are no tourist facilities. Just cabins for the diamond hunters."

"There are diamond mines?"

"Probably," she said. She had become dismissive.

"What makes it dangerous?"

"The flies."

"Biting flies? Do they carry disease?"

"No." She was downright sullen by now.

"I'd like to try it for a few days," I said, as winningly as I could. "Just to find out if I'm brave. If I get scared, I'll come right back. Give me an open flight back."

"No airport."

"Ah," said I, more winningly than ever. "So how would I get there?"

"Ship," she said, unwon. "Once a week."

Nothing rouses an attitude like an attitude. "Fine!" I said.

At least, I thought as I left the travel agency, it won't be anything like Laputa. I had read *Gulliver's Travels* as a child, in a slightly abridged and probably greatly expurgated version. My memory of it was like all my childhood memories, immediate, broken, vivid—bits of bright particularity in a vast drift of oblivion. I remembered that Laputa floated in the air, so you had to use an airship to get to it. And really I remembered little else, except that the Laputans were immortal, and that I had liked it the least of Gulliver's four travels, deciding it was *for grown-ups,* a damning quality at the time. Did the Laputans have spots, moles, something like that, which distinguished them? And were they scholars? But they grew senile, and lived on and on in incontinent idiocy—or did I imagine that? There was something nasty about them, something like that, something for grown-ups.

But I was on Yendi, where Swift's works were not in the library. I could not look it up. Instead, since I had a whole day before the ship sailed, I went to the library and looked up the Island of the Immortals.

The Central Library of Undund is a noble old building full of modern conveniences, including legemats. I asked a librarian for assistance and he brought me Postwand's *Explorations,* written about a hundred and sixty years earlier, from which I copied what follows. At the time Postwand wrote, the port city where I was staying, An Ria, had not been founded; the great wave of settlers from the east had not begun; the peoples of the coast were scattered tribes of shepherds and farmers. Postwand took a rather patronising but intelligent interest in their stories.

"Among the legends of the peoples of the West Coast," he writes, "one concerned a large island two or three days west from Undund Bay, where live *the people who never die.* All whom I asked about it were familiar with the reputation of the Island of the Immortals, and some even told me that members of

their tribe had visited the place. Impressed with the unanimity of this tale, I determined to test its veracity. When at length Vong had finished making repairs to my boat, I sailed out of the Bay and due west over the Great Sea. A following wind favored my expedition.

"About noon on the fifth day, I raised the island. Low-lying, it appeared to be at least fifty miles long from north to south.

"In the region in which I first brought the boat close to the land, the shores were entirely salt marsh. It being low tide, and the weather unbearably sultry, the putrid smell of the mud kept us well away, until at length sighting sand beaches, I sailed into a shallow bay and soon saw the roofs of a small town at the mouth of a creek. We tied up at a crude and decrepit jetty and with indescribable emotion, on my part at least, set foot on this isle reputed to hold the secret of ETERNAL LIFE."

I think I shall abbreviate Postwand; he's long-winded, and besides, he's always sneering at Vong, who seems to do most of the work and have none of the indescribable emotions. So he and Vong trudged around the town, finding it all very shabby and nothing out of the ordinary, except that there were dreadful swarms of flies. Everyone went about in gauze clothing from head to toe, and all the doors and windows had screens. Postwand assumed the flies would bite savagely, but found they didn't; they were annoying, he says, but one scarcely felt their bites, which didn't swell up or itch. He wondered if they carried some disease. He asked the islanders, who disclaimed all knowledge of disease, saying nobody ever got sick except mainlanders.

At this, Postwand got excited, naturally, and asked them if they ever died. "Of course," they said.

He does not say what else they said, but one gathers they treated him as yet another idiot from the mainland asking stupid questions. He becomes quite testy, and makes comments on their backwardness, bad manners, and execrable cookery. After a disagreeable night in a hut of some kind, he explored inland for several miles, on foot since there was no other way to get about. In a tiny village near a marsh he saw a sight that was, in his words, "proof positive that the islanders' claim of being free from disease was mere boastfulness, or something yet more sinister: for a more dreadful example of the ravages of udreba I have never seen, even in the wilds of Rotogo. The sex of the poor victim was indistinguishable; of the legs, nothing remained but stumps; the whole body was as if it had been melted in fire; only the hair, which was quite white, grew luxuriantly, long, tangled, and filthy—a crowning horror to this sad spectacle."

I looked up *udreba*. It's a disease the Yendians dread as we dread leprosy, which it resembles, though it is far more immediately dangerous; a single contact with saliva or any exudation can cause infection. There is no vaccine and no cure. Postwand was horrified to see children playing close by the udreb. He apparently lectured a woman of the village on hygiene, at which she took offense and lectured him back, telling him not to stare at people. She picked up the poor udreb "as if it were a child of five," he says, and took it into her hut. She came out with a bowl full of something, muttering loudly. At this point Vong, with whom I sympathise, suggested that it was time to leave. "I acceded to my companion's groundless apprehensions," Postwand says. They sailed away that evening.

I can't say that this account raised my enthusiasm for visiting the island. I sought some more modern information. My librarian had drifted off, the way Yendians always seemed to do. I didn't know how to use the subject catalogue, or it was even more incomprehensibly organised than our electronic subject catalogues, or there was singularly little information concerning the Island of the Immortals in the library. All I found was a treatise entitled the *Diamonds of Aya*—a name sometimes given the island. The article was too technical for the legemat; it kept leaving blanks. I couldn't understand much except that apparently there were no mines; the diamonds did not occur deep in the earth but were to be found lying on the surface of it—as I think is the case in a southern African desert on my plane. As the island of Aya was forested and swampy, its diamonds were exposed by heavy rains or mud slides in the wet season. People went and wandered around looking for them. A big one turned up just often enough to keep people coming. The islanders apparently never joined in the search. In fact, some baffled diamond hunters claimed that the natives buried diamonds when they found them. If I understood the treatise, some that had been found were immense by our standards: they were described as lumps, usually black or dark, occasionally clear, and weighing up to five pounds. Nothing was said about cutting these huge stones, what they were used for, or their market price. Evidently the Yendians didn't prize diamonds as we do. There was a lifeless, almost furtive tone to the treatise, as if it concerned something vaguely shameful.

Surely if the islanders knew anything about "the secret of ETERNAL LIFE," there'd be a bit more about them, and it, in the library?

It was mere stubbornness, or reluctance to go back to the sullen travel agent and admit my mistake, that impelled me to the docks the next morning.

I cheered up no end when I saw my ship, a charming mini-liner with about thirty pleasant staterooms. Its fortnightly round took it to several islands farther west than Aya. Its sister ship, stopping by on the homeward leg, would bring me back to the mainland at the end of my week. Or perhaps I would simply stay aboard and have a two-week cruise? That was fine with the ship's staff. They were informal, even lackadaisical, about arrangements. I had the impression that low energy and a short attention span were quite common among Yendians. But my companions on the ship were undemanding, and the cold fish salads were excellent. I spent two days on the top deck watching seabirds swoop, great red fish leap, and translucent vanewings hover over the sea.

We sighted Aya very early in the morning of the third day. At the mouth of the bay the smell of the marshes was truly discouraging; but a conversation with the ship's captain had decided me to visit Aya after all, and I disembarked.

The captain, a man of sixty or so, had assured me that there were indeed immortals on the island. They were not born immortal but contracted immortality from the bite of the island flies. It was, he thought, a virus. "You'll want to take precautions," he said. "It's rare. I don't think there's been a new case in the last hundred years—longer, maybe. But you don't want to take chances."

After pondering a while I inquired, as delicately as possible, though delicacy is hard to achieve on the translatomat, whether there weren't people who *wanted* to escape death—people who came to the island *hoping* to be bitten by one of these lively flies. Was there a drawback I did not know about, some price too high to pay even for immortality?

The captain considered my question. He was slow-spoken, unexcitable, verging on the lugubrious. "I think so," he said. He looked at me. "You can judge," he said. "After you've been there."

He would say no more. A ship's captain is a person who has that privilege.

The ship did not put into the bay, but was met out beyond the bar by a boat that took passengers ashore. The other passengers were still in their cabins. Nobody but the captain and a couple of sailors watched me (all rigged out head to foot in a suit of strong but gauzy mesh which I had rented from the ship) clamber down into the boat and wave good-bye. The captain nodded. One of the sailors waved. I was frightened. It was no help at all that I didn't know what I was frightened of.

Putting the captain and Postwand together, it sounded as if the price of immortality was the horrible disease udreba. But I really had very little evidence, and my curiosity was intense. If a virus that made you immortal turned up in my country, vast sums of money would be poured into studying it, and if it had bad effects, scientists would alter it genetically to get rid of them, and the talk shows would yatter on about it, and news anchors would pontificate about it, and the Pope would do some pontificating too, and so would all the other holy men, and meanwhile the very rich would be cornering not only the market but the supplies. And then the very rich would be even more different from you and me.

I was curious why none of this had happened. The Yendians were apparently so uninterested in their chance to be immortal that there was scarcely anything about it in the library.

But I could see, as the boat drew close to the town, that the travel agent had been a bit disingenuous. There had been hotels here—a couple of big ones, four stories. They were all visibly derelict, signs askew, windows boarded or blank.

The boatman, a shy young man, rather nice-looking as well as I could tell through his gauze envelope, said, "Hunters' lodge, ma'am?" into my translatomat. I nodded and he sailed us neatly to a small jetty at the north end of the docks. The waterfront too had seen better days. It was now sagging and forlorn, no ships, only a couple of trawlers or crabbers. I stepped up onto the dock, looking about nervously for flies; but there were none at the moment. I tipped the boatman a couple of radlo, and he was so grateful he took me up the street, a sad little street, to the diamond hunters' lodge. It consisted of eight or nine decrepit cabins managed by a dispirited woman who, speaking slowly but without any commas or periods, said to take number 4 because the screens were the best ones breakfast at eight dinner at seven eighteen radlo and did I want a lunch packed a radlo fifty extra.

All the other cabins were unoccupied. The toilet had a little, internal, eternal leak, *tink . . . tink,* which I could not find the source of. Dinner and breakfast arrived on trays, and were edible. The flies arrived with the heat of the day, plenty of them, but not the thick fearsome swarms I had expected. The screens kept them out, and the gauze suit kept them from biting. They were small, weak-looking, brownish flies.

That day and the next morning, walking about the town,

the name of which I could not find written anywhere, I felt that the Yendian tendency to depression had bottomed out here, attained nadir. The islanders were a sad people. They were listless. They were lifeless. My mind turned up that word and stared at it.

I realised I'd waste my whole week just getting depressed if I didn't rouse up my courage and ask some questions. I saw my young boatman fishing off the jetty and went to talk to him.

"Will you tell me about the immortals?" I asked him, after some halting amenities.

"Well, most people just walk around and look for them. In the woods," he said.

"No, not the diamonds," I said, checking the translatomat. "I'm not really very interested in diamonds."

"Nobody much is any more," he said. "There used to be a lot of tourists and diamond hunters. I guess they do something else now."

"But I read in a book that there are people here who live very, very long lives—who actually don't die."

"Yes," he said, placidly.

"Are there any immortal people in town? Do you know any of them?"

He checked his fishing line. "Well, no," he said. "There was a new one, way back in my grandpa's time, but it went to the mainland. It was a woman. I guess there's an old one in the village." He nodded towards the inland. "Mother saw it once."

"If you could, would you like to live a long time?"

"Sure!" he said, with as much enthusiasm as a Yendian is capable of. "You know."

"But you don't want to be immortal. You wear the fly gauze."

He nodded. He saw nothing to discuss, in all this. He was fishing with gauze gloves, seeing the world through a mesh veil. That was life.

The storekeeper told me that you could walk to the village in a day and showed me the path. My dispirited landlady packed me a lunch. I set out next morning, attended at first by thin, persistent swarms of flies. It was a dull walk across a low, damp landscape, but the sun was mild and pleasant, and the flies finally gave up. To my surprise, I got to the village before I was even hungry for lunch. The islanders must walk slowly and seldom. It had to be the right village, though, because they spoke only of one, "the village," again no name.

It was small and poor and sad: six or seven wooden huts, rather like Russian izbas, stilted up a bit to keep them from the mud. Poultry, something like guinea fowl but mud-brown, scuttled about everywhere, making soft, raucous noises. A couple of children ran away and hid as I approached.

And there, propped up next to the village well, was the figure Postwand had described, just as he had described it—legless, sexless, the face almost featureless, blind, with skin like badly burned bread, and thick, matted, filthy white hair.

I stopped, appalled.

A woman came out of the hut to which the children had run. She came down the rickety steps and walked up to me. She gestured at my translatomat, and I automatically held it out to her so she could speak into it.

"You came to see the Immortal," she said.

I nodded.

"Two radlo fifty," she said.

I got out the money and handed it to her.

"Come this way," she said. She was poorly dressed and not clean, but a fine-looking woman, thirty-five or so, with unusual decisiveness and vigor in her voice and movements.

She led me straight to the well and stopped in front of the being propped up in a legless canvas fisherman's chair next to it. I could not look at the face, nor the horribly maimed hand. The other arm ended in a black crust above the elbow. I looked away from that.

"You are looking at the Immortal of our village," the woman said in the practiced singsong of the tour guide. "It has been with us for many many centuries. For over one thousand years it has belonged to the Roya family. In this family it is our duty and pride to look after the Immortal. Feeding hours are six in the morning and six in the evening. It lives on milk and barley broth. It has a good appetite and enjoys good health with no sicknesses. It does not have udreba. Its legs were lost when there was an earthquake one thousand years ago. It was also damaged by fire and other accidents before it came into the care of the Roya family. The legend of my family says that the Immortal was once a handsome young man who made his living for many lifetimes of normal people by hunting in the marshes. This was two to three thousand years ago, it is believed. The Immortal cannot hear what you say or see you, but is glad to accept your prayers for its well-being and any offerings for its support, as it is entirely dependent on the Roya family for food and shelter. Thank you very much. I will answer questions."

After a while I said, "It can't die."

She shook her head. Her face was impassive; not unfeeling, but closed.

"You aren't wearing gauze," I said, suddenly realising this. "The children weren't. Aren't you—"

She shook her head again. "Too much trouble," she said, in a quiet, unofficial voice. "The children always tear the gauze. Anyhow, we don't have many flies. And there's only one."

It was true that the flies seemed to have stayed behind, in the town and the heavily manured fields near it.

"You mean there's only one immortal at a time?"

"Oh, no," she said. "There are others all around. In the ground. Sometimes people find them. Souvenirs. The really old ones. Ours is young, you know." She looked at the Immortal with a weary but proprietary eye, the way a mother looks at an unpromising infant.

"The diamonds?" I said. "The diamonds are immortals?"

She nodded. "After a really long time," she said. She looked away, across the marshy plain that surrounded the village, and then back at me. "A man came from the mainland, last year, a scientist. He said we ought to bury our Immortal. So it could turn to diamond, you know. But then he said it takes thousands of years to turn. All that time it would be starving and thirsty in the ground and nobody would look after it. It is wrong to bury a person alive. It is our family duty to look after it. And no tourists would come."

It was my turn to nod. The ethics of this situation were beyond me. I accepted her choice.

"Would you like to feed it?" she asked, apparently liking something about me, for she smiled at me.

226

"No," I said, and I have to admit that I burst into tears.

She came closer and patted my shoulder.

"It is very, very sad," she said. She smiled again. "But the children like to feed it," she said. "And the money helps."

"Thank you for being so kind," I said, wiping my eyes, and I gave her another five radlo, which she took gratefully. I turned around and walked back across the marshy plains to the town, where I waited four more days until the sister ship came by from the west, and the nice young man took me out in the boat, and I left the Island of the Immortals, and soon after that I left the Yendian plane.

We are a carbon-based life-form, as the scientists say, but how a human body could turn to diamond I do not know, unless through some spiritual factor, perhaps the result of genuinely endless suffering.

Perhaps "diamond" is only a name the Yendians give these lumps of ruin, a kind of euphemism.

I am still not certain what the woman in the village meant when she said, "There's only one." She was not referring to the immortals. She was explaining why she didn't protect herself or her children from the flies, why she found the risk not worth the bother. It is possible that she meant that among the swarms of flies in the island marshes there is only one fly, one immortal fly, whose bite infects its victim with eternal life.

Confusions of Uñi

One *hears of* planes where no one should go, planes no one should visit even briefly. Sometimes in the dreary bustle of airport bars men at the next table talk in low voices, saying things like, "I told him what the Gnegn did to MacDowell," or, "He thought he could handle it on Vavizzua." Then a harsh, shrill, enormously amplified voice blats out, "Flight onteen to Hhuhh is now boarding at gate throighty-six," or, "Shimbleglood Rrggrrggrr to a white courtesy phone please," drowning out all other voices and driving sleep and hope from the poor souls who droop across blue plastic seats with steel legs bolted to the floor trying to catch a little rest between planes; and the words of the men at the next table are lost. Of course the men may merely be boasting to increase the glamor of their lives;

228

surely if the Gnegn or Vavizzua were truly dangerous, the Interplanary Agency would warn people to stay away—as they warn them to stay off Zuehe.

It's well known that the Zuehe plane is unusually tenuous. Visitors of ordinary mass and solidity are in danger of breaking through the delicate meshes of Zuehan reality, damaging a whole neighborhood in the process and ruining the happiness of their hosts. The affectionate, intimate relationships so important to the Zuehe may be permanently strained and even torn apart by the destructive weight of an ignorant and uncaring intruder. Meantime, the intruder suffers no more from such an accident than an abrupt return to his own plane, sometimes in a peculiar position or upside down, which is embarrassing, but after all at an airport one is among strangers and so shame has little power.

We'd all like to see the moonstone towers of Nezihoa, as pictured in Rornan's *Planary Guide,* the endless steppes of mist, the dim forests of the Sezu, the beautiful men and women of the Zuehe, with their slightly translucent clothes and bodies, their pale grey eyes, their hair the color of tarnished silver, so fine the hand does not know when it touches it. It is sad that so lovely a plane must not be visited, fortunate that those who have glimpsed it have been able to describe it for us. Still, some people go there. Ordinarily selfish people justify their invasion of Zuehe by the familiar expedient of considering themselves as not like all those *other* people who go to Zuehe and spoil it. Extremely selfish people go to Zuehe to boast about it, precisely because it is fragile, destructible, therefore a trophy.

The Zuehe themselves are far too gentle, reticent, and vague to forbid anybody entry. Verbs in their cloudy language do not even have an indicative mode, let alone an imperative. They use only the conditional. They have a thousand ways of saying maybe, perhaps, lest, although, if . . . but not yes, not no.

So at the usual entry point the Interplanary Agency has set up, instead of a hotel, a net, a large, strong, nylon net. In it anybody arriving on Zuehe, even unintentionally, is caught, sprayed with sheep-dip, given a pamphlet containing a straightforward warning in 442 languages, and sent straight back to their own, more durable though less enticing plane, where the Agency makes sure that they arrive upside down.

I have only been to one plane I really wouldn't recommend to anybody and to which I shall certainly never return. I'm not sure it is exactly dangerous. I am no judge of danger. Only the brave can be that. Thrills and chills which to some people are the spice of life take the flavor right out of mine. When I'm frightened, food is sawdust—sex, with its vulnerability of body and soul, is the last thing I want—words are meaningless, thought incoherent, love paralysed. Cowardice of this degree is, I know, uncommon. Many people would have to hang by their teeth from a frayed cord suspended by a paper clip from a leaking hot air balloon over the Grand Canyon in order to feel what I feel standing on the third step of a stepladder trying to put millet in the bird feeder. And they'd find the terror exhilarating and take up skydiving as soon as their broken pelvis mended. Whereas I descend slowly from the stepladder, clutching at the porch rail, and swear I'll never go above six inches again.

So I don't fly any more than I absolutely have to, and when I do get trapped in airports I don't go looking for the dangerous planes, but for the peaceful ones, the dull, ordinary, complicated ones, where I can be not frightened out of my wits but just ordinarily frightened, the way cowards are most of the time.

Waiting out a missed connection in the Denver airport, I fell into conversation with a friendly couple who'd been to Uñi. They told me it was "a nice place." As they were elderly, he laden with an expensive camcorder and other electronic impediments, she wearing pantyhose and deeply unadventurous white wedgie sandals, I thought they wouldn't have said that about anywhere dangerous. That was stupid of me. I should have been warned by the fact that they weren't good at description. "Lot going on there," the man said. "But all pretty much like here. Not one of those *foreign* foreign places." The wife added, "It's a storybook country! Just like things you see on TV."

Even that didn't alert me.

"The weather's very nice," the wife said. The husband amended, "Changeable."

That was OK. I had a light raincoat with me. My flight to Memphis wasn't for an hour and half yet. I went to Uñi.

I checked into the Interplanary Inn. WELCOME TO OUR FRIENDS FROM THE ASTRAL PLANE! said a sign on the desk. A pale, heavyset, redheaded woman behind the desk gave me a translatomat and a self-guiding map of the town, but also pointed out to me the large placard: EXPERIENCE OUR VIRTUAL REALITY TOUR OF BEAUTIFUL UÑI EVERY TWENTY IZ!MIT.

"You must do," she said.

In general I evade "virtual experiences," which were always recorded in better weather than it is today and which take the novelty out of everything you're about to see without giving any real information. But two pale, heavyset clerks ushered me in such a determinedly friendly fashion to the VR cubicle that I had not the courage to protest. They helped me insert my head into the helmet, wrap the bodywrap around my body, and slip my legs and arms into the long stocking-gloves. And then I sat there quite alone for what felt like at least a quarter of an hour, waiting for the show to start, resisting claustrophobia, watching the colors inside my eyes, and wondering how long an iz!mit was. Or was the singular iz!m? Or was plural number shown by a prefix, so that the singular would be z!mit? Nothing whatever happened, speculative grammar palled, and I said the hell with it. I slipped out of the VR swaddle, walked past the clerks with guilty nonchalance, and got outside among the potted shrubs. The potted shrubs in front of hotels are the same on every plane.

I looked at my self-guiding map and set out to visit the Art Museum, which had three stars. The day was cool and sunny. The town, built mostly of grey stone with red tile roofs, looked old, settled, prosperous. People went about their business paying no attention to me. The Uñiats seemed mostly to be heavyset, white-skinned, and red-haired. All of them wore coats, long skirts, and thick boots.

I found the Art Museum in its little park and went in. The paintings were mostly of heavyset, white-skinned, red-haired women with no clothes on, though some wore boots. They were well painted, but they didn't do much for me. I was on my way out when I got drawn into a discussion. Two people, both men I thought, though it was hard to say given the coats, skirts, and boots, stood arguing in front of a painting of a plump red-haired female wearing nothing but boots on a flowered couch. As I passed, one of them turned to me and said, or so my trans-

latomat rendered what he said, "If the figure's a central design element in the counterplay of blocks and masses, you can't reduce
the painting to a study of indirect light on surfaces, can you?"

He, or she, asked the question so simply, directly, and ur-
gently that I could not merely say, "Excuse me?" or shake my
head and pretend to be uncomprehending. I looked again at the
painting and after a moment said, "Well, not usefully, perhaps."

"But listen to the woodwinds," said the other man, and I realised that the ambient music was an orchestral piece of some
kind, dominated at the moment by plangent wind instruments,
oboes perhaps, or bassoons in a high register. "The change of
key is definitive," the man said, a little too loudly. The person sitting behind us leaned forward and hissed, "Shh!" while a person
in the row in front of us turned around and glared. Embarrassed,
I sat very still throughout the rest of the piece, which was quite
pretty, though the changes of key, or something of that kind—
the only way I can recognise a change of key is when I cry without knowing why I am crying—gave it a certain incoherence. I
was surprised when a tenor, or possibly a contralto, whom I had
not previously noticed, stood up and began to sing the main
theme in a powerful voice, ending on a long high note to wild
applause from the audience in the big auditorium. They shouted
and clapped and demanded an encore. But a gust of wind blowing in from the high hills to the west across the village square
made all the trees shiver and bow, and looking up at the clouds
streaming overhead I realised a storm was imminent. The clouds
darkened from moment to moment, another great blast of wind
struck, whirling up dust and leaves and litter, and I thought I'd
better put on my raincoat. But I had checked it at the cloakroom

in the Art Museum. My translatomat was clipped to my jacket lapel, but the self-guiding map had been in my raincoat pocket. I went to the desk in the tiny station building and asked when the next train left, and the one-eyed man behind the narrow iron grating said, "We do not have trains now."

I turned to see the empty tracks stretching away under the vast arched roof of the station, track after track, each with its number and its gate. Here and there was a luggage cart, and a single distant passenger straying idly down a long platform, but no trains. "I need my raincoat," I said, in a kind of panic.

"Try Lost and Found," the one-eyed clerk said, and busied himself with forms and schedules. I walked across the great hollow space of the station towards the entrance. Beyond a restaurant and a coffee bar I found the Lost and Found. I went into it and said, "I checked my raincoat at the Art Museum, but I have lost the Art Museum."

The statuesque red-haired woman at the counter said, "Wait a minute" in a bored voice, rummaged a bit, and shoved a map across the counter. "There," she said, pointing at a square with a white, plump, red-nailed finger. "That's the Art Museum."

"But I don't know where I am. Where this is. This village."

"Here," she said, pointing out another square on the map. It seemed to be ten or twelve streets from the Art Museum. "Better go while the conformation lasts. Stormy today."

"Can I take the map?" I asked pitifully. She nodded.

I went out into the city streets, so mistrustful that I walked with short steps, as if the pavement might turn into an abyss before my feet, or a cliff face rise up before me, or the street crossing turn into the deck of a ship at sea. Nothing happened. The

wide, level streets of the city crossed each other at regular intervals, treeless, quiet. The electric buses and taxis made little noise,
and there were no private cars. I walked on. The map took me
right back to the Art Museum, which I thought had had green-
and-white marble steps instead of black slate ones, but other
things about it were as I remembered. In general, I have a poor
memory. I went in and asked at the cloakroom for my raincoat.
While the black-haired, silver-eyed girl with thin black lips was
looking for it, I wondered why I had asked, at the train station,
when the next train left. Where had I thought I was going? All I
had wanted was my coat at the Art Museum. If there had been a
train, would I have taken it? Where would I have got off?

As soon as I had my coat, I hurried back through the steep,
cobbled streets lined with charming balconied houses and
crowded with the slender, almost skeletal, black-lipped people of
Uñi, towards the Interplanary Hotel to demand an explanation.
It was probably something in the air, I thought, as the fog thick-
ened, hiding the mountains above the town and the peaked roofs
of the houses on the hills. Maybe people on Uñi smoked something hallucinatory, or there was some pollen or something in the
air or in the fog that affected the mind, confused the senses, or—
a nasty thought—deleted stretches of memory, so that things
seemed to happen without sequence and you couldn't remember
how you'd got where you were or what had happened in between. And having a poor memory, I might not be sure whether
I had lost parts of it or not. It was like dreaming in some respects, but I was certainly not dreaming, only confused and increasingly alarmed, so that despite the damp cold I didn't stop to

put on my raincoat, but hurried shivering onward through the forest.

I smelled wood smoke, sweet and sharp in the wet air, and presently saw a gleam of light through the twilight mist that gathered almost palpable among the trees. A woodcutter's hut stood just off the path, a shadowy bit of kitchen garden beside it, the red-gold glow of firelight in the low, small-paned window, smoke drifting up from the chimney, a lonesome, homely sight. I knocked. After a minute an old man opened the door. He was bald, and had an enormous wen or wart on his nose and a frying pan in his hand, in which sausages were sizzling cheerily. "You can have three wishes," he said.

"I wish to find the Interplanary Hotel," I said.

"That is the wish you cannot have," the old man said. "Don't you want to wish that the sausages were growing out of the end of my nose?"

After a brief pause for thought, I said, "No."

"So, what do you wish for, besides the way to the Interplanary Hotel?"

I thought again. I said, "When I was twelve or thirteen, I used to plan what I'd wish for if they gave me three wishes. I thought I'd wish, *I wish that having lived well to the age of eighty-five and having written some very good books, I may die quietly, knowing that all the people I love are happy and in good health.* I knew that this was a stupid, disgusting wish. Pragmatic. Selfish. A coward's wish. I knew it wasn't fair. They would never allow it to be one of my three wishes. Besides, having wished it, what would I do with the other two wishes? So then I'd think, with the other two I could wish that everybody in the world was happier, or that they'd stop fighting wars, or that they'd wake up tomorrow morning feeling really good and be kind to everybody else all day, no, all year, no, forever, but then I'd realise I didn't really believe in any of these wishes as anything but wishes. So long as they were wishes they were fine, even useful, but they couldn't go any further than being wishes. By nothing I do can I attain a goal beyond my reach, as King Yudhishthira said when he found heaven wasn't all he'd hoped for. There are gates the bravest horse can't jump. If wishes were horses, I'd have a whole herd of them, roan and buckskin, lovely wild horses, never bridled, never broken, galloping over the plains past red mesas and blue mountains. But cowards ride rocking horses made of wood with painted eyes, and back and forth they go, back and forth in one place on the playroom floor, back and forth, and all the plains and mesas and mountains are only in the rider's eyes. So never mind about the wishes. Give me a sausage, please."

We ate together, the old man and I. The sausages were excellent, so were the mashed potatoes and fried onions. I could not have wished for a better supper. After it we sat in companionable silence for a bit, looking at the fire, and then I thanked him for his hospitality and asked him for directions to the Interplanary Hotel.

"It's a wild night," he said, rocking in his rocking chair.

"I have to be in Memphis tomorrow morning," I said.

"Memphis," he said thoughtfully, or perhaps he said "Memfish." He rocked a bit and said, "Ah, well, then. Better go east."

And as at that moment a whole group of people erupted from an inner room I had not previously noticed, bluish-skinned silver-haired people dressed in tuxedos, off-the-shoulder ball gowns, and tiny pointy shoes, arguing shrilly, laughing loudly, making exaggerated gestures, batting their eyes, each holding a cocktail glass containing an oily liquid and one embalmed green olive, I did not feel like staying any longer, but plunged out into the night, which evidently was going to be wild only in the old man's cottage, because out here on the seashore it was quite still, a half moon shining over the placid black water that sighed and rustled softly on the broad, curving beach.

Having no idea which direction east was, I began walking to the right, as east generally feels like the right to me and west feels like the left, which must mean that I face north a good deal. The water was inviting; I took off my shoes and stockings and waded in the cool come-and-go of shallow waves on the sand. It was so peaceful that I was not at all prepared for the burst of loud noise, fiercely bright light, and hot tomato soup that surged briefly around me, knocking me off my feet and half stifling me, as I staggered up onto the deck of a ship plunging through sheets of rain over a choppy, grey sea full of whitecaps or the heads of porpoises, I could not tell which. An enormous voice from the bridge bellowed incomprehensible orders and the even more enormous voice of the ship's siren lamented vastly through the rain and mist, warning off the icebergs. "I wish I was at the Interplanary Hotel!" I shouted, but my puny cry was annihilated by the clamor and din all about me, and I had never believed in three wishes anyway. My clothes were soaked with tomato soup and rain and I was most uncomfortable, until a lightning bolt—green lightning, I had read of it but never seen it—zapped with a sizzle as of huge frying sausages down through the grey commotion not five yards from me and with a tremendous crash split the deck right down the middle. Fortunately we had just that moment struck an iceberg, which wedged itself into the cloven ship. I climbed the rail and stepped off the terrifying pitch of the deck onto the ice. From the iceberg I watched the two halves of the ship slant farther and farther apart as they slowly sank. All the people who had rushed up on deck wore blue bathing suits, trunks for the men, Olympic style for the women. Some of the suits had gold stripes, the officers' suits evidently, for the people with gold-striped blue suits shouted orders which the ones in plain blue suits promptly obeyed, letting down six lifeboats, three to a side, and climbing into them in an orderly fashion. The last one in was a man with so many gold stripes on his bathing trunks that you could hardly see they were blue. As he stepped into the lifeboat, both halves of the ship sank quietly. The lifeboats fell into line and began to row away among the white-nosed porpoises.

"Wait," I called, "wait! What about me?"

They did not look back. The boats disappeared quickly in the roiling gloom over the icy, porpoiseful water. There was nothing for it but to climb my iceberg and see what I could see. As I clambered over the humps and pinnacles of ice, I thought of Peter Pan on his rock, saying, "To die will be a great adventure," or that's how I remembered what he said. I had always thought that that was very brave of Peter Pan, definitely a constructive way to look at dying, and perhaps even true. But I didn't particularly want to find out whether it was true or not, just now. Just now, I wanted to get back to the Interplanary Hotel. But alas, when I reached the summit of the iceberg, no hotel was visible. I saw nothing but grey sea, porpoises, grey mists and clouds, and darkness slowly thickening.

Everything else, everywhere else, had changed quickly into somewhere else. Why didn't this? Why didn't the iceberg become a wheat field, or an oil refinery, or a pissoir? Why was I stuck on it? Wasn't there something I could do? Click my heels and say, "I want to be in Kansas"? What was *wrong* with this plane, anyhow? A storybook world, indeed! My feet were very cold by now, and only the lingering warmth of the tomato soup kept my clothes from freezing in the bitter wind that whined over the surface of the ice. I had to move. I had to do something. I started trying to dig a hole in the ice with my hands and heels, breaking off projections, kicking till big flakes came loose and I could pry them up and toss them away. As they flew out over the sea they looked like gulls or white butterflies. A big help that was. I was by now very angry, so angry that the iceberg began to melt around me, steaming and fizzing faintly, and I sank into it like a hot poker, red-hot with fury, and yelled at the two pale people who were hastily stripping the long stocking-gloves off my legs and arms, "What the hell do you think you're doing?"

They were terribly embarrassed and worried. They were afraid I had gone mad, afraid I was going to sue their Interplanary Inn, afraid I would say bad things about Uñi on other planes. They did not know what had gone wrong with the Virtual Reality Experience of Beautiful Uñi, although clearly something had. They had called for their programmer.

When he came—wearing nothing but blue swim trunks and horn-rimmed glasses—he barely examined the machine. He declared it was in perfect order. He asserted that my "confusion" had been due to an unfortunate semi-overlap of frequencies, a kind of mental moiré effect, caused by something unusual in my brainwaves interacting with their program. An anomaly, he said. The effect of a resistance, he said. His tone was accusatory. I got angry all over again and told him and the clerks that if their damned machine malfunctioned, they shouldn't blame me but either fix it or shut it down and let tourists experience beautiful Uñi in their own solid, anomalous, resistant flesh.

The manager now arrived, a heavyset, white-skinned, red-headed woman with no clothes on at all, only boots. The clerks wore minidresses and boots. The person vacuuming the lobby was a veritable mass of skirts, trousers, jackets, scarves, and veils. It appeared that the higher a Uñiat's rank, the less they wore. But I had no interest now in their folkways. I glared at the manager. She smarmed halfheartedly and made the kind of threatening apology-bargain such people make, which means take what we offer if you know what's good for you. There would be no charge for my stay at the inn or at any hotel on Uñi, I would have free rail passage to picturesque J!ma, complimentary tickets to the museums, the circus, the sausage factory, all sorts of stuff, which she reeled off mechanically till I broke in. No thanks, I'd had quite enough of Uñi and was leaving right now. I had to catch my flight to Memfish.

"How?" she said, with an unpleasant smile.

At that simple question a flood of terror washed through me like meltwater from the iceberg, paralysing my body, stopping breath and thought.

I knew how I'd got here, how I'd gone to other planes—by waiting at the airport, of course.

But the airport was on my plane, not this plane. I did not know *how to get back to the airport.*

I stood frozen, as they say.

Fortunately the manager was only too eager to be rid of me. What the translatomat had translated as "How?" had been a conventional phrase on the order of "How regrettable," which the manager's fleshy but tight lips had truncated. My cowardice, leaping at the false signal, had stopped my brain, chopped off my memory, just as the mere fear of forgetting the name ensures that I will forget the name of anyone I have to introduce to anyone else.

"The waiting room is this way," the manager said, and escorted me back across the lobby, her bare haunches moving with a heavy, malevolent waggle.

Of course all Interplanary inns and hotels have a waiting room exactly like an airport, with rows of plastic chairs bolted to the floor, and a horrible diner with no seats which is closed but reeks of stale beef fat, and a flabby man with a nose cold overflowing from the chair next to you, and a display of expected flight arrivals and departures which flickers by so fast you never can be quite sure you've found your connecting plane among the thousands of listings, although when you do catch its number they seem to have changed the gate, which means that you need to be in a different concourse, so that your anxiety soon rises to an effective level—and there you are back in the Denver airport sitting on a plastic chair bolted to the floor next to a fat, phlegmy man reading a magazine called *Successful Usury* amid the smell of stale beef fat, the wails of a miserable two-year-old, and the hugely amplified voice of a woman whom

I visualise as a heavyset, white-skinned, naked redhead in boots announcing that flight four-enty to Memfish has been canceled.

I was grateful to be back on my plane. I did not want to go east now. I wanted to go west. I found a flight to beautiful, peaceful, sane Los Engeles and went there. In the hotel there I had a long, very hot bath. I know people die of heart attacks in very hot baths, but I took the risk.

URSULA K. LE GUIN lives in Portland, Oregon. Winner of the National Book Award, the Harold D. Vursell Memorial Award from the American Academy of Arts and Letters, and the PEN/Malamud Award, she is a novelist, poet, and essayist; and she has written more than one hundred short stories.

ERIC BEDDOWS has won the Amelia Frances Howard-Gibbon Award and the Governor General's Literary Award, among others.